International Praise for Alison Moore

"Dense, complex, thought-provoking, [*Death and the Seaside*] manages to be at once a fairytale and a philosophical treatise, high-octane thriller and literary interrogation. Like the dreams that haunt Bonnie's night-times, it holds its secrets close, and repays careful rereading. The end of the novel, abrupt and death-haunted, feels as neat and tight as a key in a lock, and sheds light on the mysteries that have gone before."—Sarah Crown, *The Guardian* Book of the Day

"As the parallel stories unpack these two [protagonists'] respective pasts, talismans of memory seem to uncannily connect them: Venus flytraps, the smell of a certain perfume, replica lighthouses that both keep as protective charms. Ms. Moore has written a short, bleak, atmospheric book full of such strange symbols that ... suddenly come aglow with meaning."—*Wall Street Journal*

"The tales collected in *The Pre-War House* ... pick at psychological scabs in a register both wistful and brutal."—*Times Literary Supplement*

"There is an insistent, rhythmic quality to Moore's writing, and a dark imagination at work."—*Daily Mail*

"[There's] a quiet sense of sadness that dogs these characters. As they navigate their lives, Moore slowly unearths their essential fears, regrets, and unmet desires, producing a subdued and beautiful fe reader ruminating long afte lection."—*Kirkus Reviews*

DEATH AND THE SEASIDE

DEATH
AND THE
SEASIDE

ALISON
MOORE

BIBLIOASIS
WINDSOR, ONTARIO

Library and Archives Canada Cataloguing in Publication

Moore, Alison, 1971-, author
    Death and the seaside / Alison Moore.

Previously published: Cromer, Norfolk: Salt Publishing, 2016.

Issued in print and electronic formats.
ISBN 978-1-77196-275-9 (softcover).--ISBN 978-1-77196-276-6 (ebook)

        I. Title.

PR6113.O553D43 2019   823'.92   C2018-904458-6
                                            C2018-904459-4

Readied for the press by Daniel Wells
Typeset by Chris Andrechek
Cover designed by Zoe Norvell

PRINTED AND BOUND IN THE USA

To Nick Royle

undertow • n. = undercurrent • n. 1 a current of water below the surface and moving in a different direction from any surface current. 2 an underlying feeling or influence.

—Oxford English Dictionary

I

I

Sometimes, Susan woke to find that her limbs were dead. Her arm would be flung back, bent beneath her head, the blood stopped, and she would have to move it with her other hand, the dead weight unsettling her, as if she had woken to find a ten-pound leg of lamb lying on her pillow; or one leg would be lying lifeless beneath the other, and she would have to lift the numb leg with both hands, holding it under the thigh and hanging it over the side of her bed like a Christmas stocking that wanted filling. This had been happening to her for as long as she could remember.

This morning, it was her right leg. Sitting on the edge of her mattress, she stretched her blood-starved toes, the nasty comfort of pins and needles bringing her leg fizzing back to life.

She had no curtains at her window, nothing to buffer the daylight in those first few minutes of being awake. She had been promised curtains but, in the meantime, it did not bother her too much. Her room was in the attic, so it was not like anyone walking by could see in. Each morning, she woke to see the window framing the bare sky. The lack of curtains only troubled her if she woke in the night and saw the cold window with all that darkness outside, that big black rectangle in the middle of the long wall.

Her cigarettes were on the windowsill. She stood, testing her foot, feeling only a residual tingling, like froth left popping on the sand when a wave pulls away. She crossed the room and opened the window, letting in the brisk sea air. Leaning on the windowsill, she lit a cigarette. She looked out at the quiet street and the churning waters beyond it.

In the coming week, there would be a bonfire on the beach; there was a poster advertising it on the wall in the pub. They would burn the old fishing boats too, like a sacrificial offering on a funeral pyre.

She smoked her cigarette down to the butt and blew the smoke outside, blowing it downwards, though it drifted up. The slabbed pavement reminded her of a dream she'd had when she was small, in which she jumped from her bedroom window to the patio slabs below and sank, very comfortably, into the ground, as if she were Mr Soft, as if nothing could hurt her. 'It wouldn't be like that though,' her mum had said, in the kitchen in the morning. 'You'd be lucky just to break your legs.'

Susan let go of her cigarette end and watched it fall to the pavement. She thought of that thing about a feather and a brick descending at exactly the same speed, or a ton of feathers and a ton of bricks. That was in a vacuum though, or on the moon or something. The butt hit the ground and Susan closed the window.

She got dressed, pulling on skinny jeans patched at the knees, and a thin, blue jumper with suede patches on the elbows. She was lanky, all legs, like the harvestmen that so unnerved her. If a predator got hold of a harvestman's leg, the harvestman could just detach it, as if it were a joke leg. It made Susan think of the fake limbs that she had seen used in

4

art and magic, to create an illusion or just to give someone a fright. She thought of the rubber hand deception, where the imitation hand began to feel like a person's real hand. The harvestman's leg was not a fake though; the escaping harvestman left the abandoned limb twitching in the predator's jaw. Since childhood, animals with spindly legs and backwards knees had set Susan's teeth on edge. She remembered seeing an emu at the zoo. Something about the way it ran, the way its legs bent the wrong way, had made her cry.

She left the room and made her way downstairs. Usually, she would have gone straight through to the bar and started work, but it was a Monday so the pub was closed and this was Susan's day off. There were boxes of bar snacks at the foot of the stairs. She took a packet of crisps and left through the back door.

She had come into the Hook on her first day here in Seatown. It was summer, and she had been thinking that until she found her feet she might sleep on the beach, but when she stood on the esplanade, looking out to sea, it occurred to her that the water was likely to come all the way to the sea wall, and some way up it; she might be spending the night on the seabed. Just behind her was the Hook, and from it had come a smell of warm food that made her feel hungry. She went inside, and saw on the bar a jolly polystone pig wearing a chef's hat and coat and holding in its cloven hooves a carving knife and a chalkboard advertising the special: ham and chips; and she saw on the wall, handwritten on a piece of paper, an advert for a room above the pub. As it happened, the landlady also wanted bar staff, and as no one but Susan had applied for the job or asked about the room, she acquired both and moved in the same day. Each morning, when she started work, she asked about the lack of curtains. 'They're coming,' she was told. 'Your curtains are coming.'

Susan ate her crisps as she wandered along the esplanade, past the signs that said 'NO CYCLING', 'NO DOGS ON THE ESPLANADE OR THE BEACH', and, at the top of the slope that went down to the beach, 'NO DISABLED ACCESS'. The fresh air in her lungs made her want another cigarette, so she smoked while she walked. The tide was coming in. She made her way to the amusements, where they were still advertising for someone to work in the change booth. Every time the manager saw her, he shouted to her, from the confines of the booth, 'This could be you!' The booth was perhaps three feet wide by three feet deep, and more than six feet tall with perspex windows on three sides. Sitting in there would make her feel like she was in one of those animatronic fortune-telling machines, like Zoltar, but at least not like Economy Zoltar whose booth was only two feet square and who had no head or arm movement. She would feel like a spider caught under a glass.

At lunchtime, Susan left the amusements with empty pockets. Sometimes, here on the coast, the force of the wind when she met it head-on, when it whistled past her ears and whipped back her short, brown hair, made her think of how it would feel to ride her motorbike without a helmet on, or to freefall. But just now, there was a lull, and she stopped to smoke a cigarette on the esplanade, leaning on the railings, facing the sea.

She had been desperate to get away from home. Even when she was little, she had run away from home, just for the fun of it. That had got her a stinging slap on her bare legs, and her mum had said, 'You've got worse than that coming your way if you ever do it again.' But then her mum had rolled her eyes and said, 'You're just like me.' Her mum had gone down to Gretna Green in her teens, to marry her boyfriend without her parents' blessing. 'You're making a mistake,' they had said, but that just made her want him more. They had been right though, about Susan's dad; Susan's mum had made a mistake, a bad choice. Maybe it ran in the family.

Susan had come south on her motorbike, racing down with the open road ahead of her, thinking about her mum on her way to Gretna Green, her future a great unknown, and about her granddad, who had lied about his age so that he could go off and fight in the war. 'He just couldn't wait,' said her mum. He went to Ypres, and spent the rest of his long life confined to a wheelchair.

Susan's grandmother always believed that travelling south was easier than travelling north because south was 'downhill' on the map, as if anyone trying to go north without concentrating risked rolling all the way back down; as if, in fact, gravity could make anyone tumble down at any moment.

Susan remembered her first sight of Seatown. It had been getting late as she approached; the sun was going down. It looked like someone had set fire to something; it was like a house on fire on the horizon, except bigger than that: it was as if someone was burning everything they owned. She had headed towards it.

She came from a small village surrounded by countryside. She had seen the newborn lambs in the field in the spring before she left; she had got away before that moment in the summer when the lambs were taken away in the lorry. She hated the thought of them going into the lorry with no idea what was coming and no way to avoid their fate anyway. She hated seeing the lorry that pulled up outside the chicken shed with 'EAT BRITISH CHICKEN' printed on the back. Susan wondered if she would make it home for Christmas. On Boxing Day, the hunt rode out, despite the fox-hunting ban. Her dad used to go with them, before he fell from his galloping horse and lost the use of his legs.

Susan took out her mobile phone and looked at the screen. The signal here came and went. There was no signal right now. Sometimes she spent ages thumbing long texts to her parents, which she then could not send. Perhaps she should change her provider. She wrote another text now, even though it would only sit in her outbox with the others until a signal could be found. She kept having to stop and undo what the predictive text function inserted. Some of the sentences that predictive text wanted to construct looked like the strange non sequiturs of someone who was losing their mind. She wondered how predictive text worked. Did her phone make predictions on the basis of texts that she had previously written? Was she herself responsible for these peculiarities? Or did the odd suggestions come from a programmer? Her granddad thought that someone managed his answerphone messages, someone in a call centre, like a switchboard operator; he got cross when they tampered with his saved messages, when they deleted something without asking.

Susan signed off her text with an 'x' and then waited for the message to fail to send. She smoked her cigarette down to the filter and dropped it, flattening it with the toe of her sandal. She walked on, back towards the Hook, outside which she kept her motorbike. She knew she ought to get some proper motorbike leathers, and boots with toe protection and ankle, heel and shin armour. Her mum had warned her that she went too fast, that she would end up hitting the tarmac at so many miles per hour and then she'd have pins in her legs, 'if you're lucky', she said. She ought at least to get some warmer footwear for the coming winter.

Susan went back inside the pub and up to her room, where she flopped down onto her unmade bed, pulled the blanket over her, and nodded off.

She dreamt that she was having difficulty walking. When she woke up, blinking in the afternoon light, she remembered the dream; she knew it was just a dream but she made a cautious effort to move her legs anyway, just in case. She did not understand what the dream meant—everything in dreams seemed to mean something else.

Sitting up, she noticed a square of paper on the carpet over by the door—a letter, she thought, or a message, that had been posted through the gap underneath the door. She walked over and picked up the scrap of paper, but when she looked at it she found that it was blank; although perhaps there was the faintest suggestion of something there, as if it had been photocopied almost to oblivion. She opened the door and peered outside but there was no one there, and no one on the stairs. She turned again to the piece of paper, and she almost thought that she might be able to make out a message after all, or just a word, but even as she looked, her sense of that dim outline disappeared, like a shadow when the sun slips behind a cloud.

2

E ARLY IN THE new year, when it was still bitter outside and Bonnie was approaching thirty, she began looking for a cheap flat. She had been living in her parents' house for years, and even though she had lived away from home before, she had never lived alone.

In her early twenties, after a gap year that had turned into three, all spent under her parents' roof, her mother had insisted that she go away to university, if she could still find one that would take her. And so she had gone to university, although it was not, as her father had pointed out, a proper university; it was not a good university. She majored in English, because it had always been her best subject and because she had managed to get a B at A level. It was also her native language.

She had got a room in halls of residence, sharing with another girl. Bonnie's roommate kept a diary. She wrote in it every night and stowed it under her mattress when she went to sleep. The first time Bonnie's roommate left the diary out on the bed while she went to the bathroom, Bonnie had been unable to resist reading it; she had opened it up and seen her own name written there, and 'weird', or something like that—she could never remember exactly what it said, exactly what she was. She had shut the diary quickly, got into bed and pretended to be asleep when the girl came back. The diary was left out another time or two after that, but Bonnie never looked in it again.

After halls, she had lived in a shared house, where one of the other students, behind the closed door of his bedroom, used to chant every day before breakfast, 'I am the master of my fate.' He repeated it three times every morning without fail, before swaggering out to start his day. Another of the students used to leave photocopied leaflets lying around where they might be seen, picked up and read. The leaflets said things like: 'God Will Save You'. Bonnie never heard him say a word, this student. If he was in the house, he stayed in his room; Bonnie only knew that he had been in the kitchen or the lounge or the bathroom because of the trail of leaflets he left behind him, like a trail of breadcrumbs laid so that no one would be lost.

In her first term, in An Introduction to English Literature, she heard about the death of the Author, and at first she wondered who they meant, and then she realised that it was all of them, all the authors, and Bonnie thought fleetingly of the dodo. And what was more, asserted Barthes, the Author *enters into his own death*, or her own death, thought Bonnie, who had just started writing herself. She had a vivid memory of the lecturer standing in the lecture theatre saying all this, although over time it had merged with another memory, of her mother coming into a room and saying that Bonnie's grandmother had died. 'She wanted to go,' said her mother. 'She was ready.' There had been a funeral, of course, a week later, and at this funeral Bonnie's mother had asked after somebody's husband, forgetting that he had died; and then somebody else, who Bonnie's mother was certain had died, came round with a plate of sandwiches.

After a few years of literary criticism, Bonnie had found that she could no longer read a story without seeing it through a lens of critical analysis, as if there were always some underlying meaning that you might miss if you were not paying attention. And at the same time, she began to see the real world in terms of narrative; she saw stories and symbolism everywhere. She found it all exhausting, and left her course—which her father had called a Mickey Mouse degree anyway—before taking her final exams or completing her dissertation.

On quitting university, she had moved home again, and her father had said to her mother, 'What did you expect?' Bonnie had been living with her parents ever since, and doing casual work. In her spare time, she sat in her old bed-room, at the same desk she had once used for her school-work, and wrote stories, or tried to. She had come to a halt in her current one, in which her protagonist had moved to the seaside and taken a room above a pub. Bonnie had got as far as her protagonist finding a message that had been pushed under the door of her room, but when she looked at it, it was blank, any message or sense of meaning evaporating before her eyes, the way even the most vivid dream could slip away as you woke, so that in moments it went from something that felt real to something that could not even be recalled. Now Bonnie did not know what to do, what might happen next. But anyway, she had put the story away. She would have to clear her desk and empty her drawers, having been told by her parents, as the big three-zero approached, that it was time for her to move out.

Although she had been asked to leave home, Bonnie had no reason to leave town. She had her jobs, and no promise of any-thing better elsewhere. She searched through the Homeseeker section of the local newspaper and found a ground-floor flat available to rent, in a terraced house at one end of Slash Lane.

'I'm not sure I like the sound of Slash Lane,' said her mother. 'It doesn't sound safe.'

'It's just a name, Mum,' said Bonnie, although she did remember how driving up Carsick Hill Road in Sheffield always made her feel queasy, and she wondered if she would ever feel comfortable walking along Slash Lane on her own in the dark.

She arranged to view the Slash Lane property, and was met outside the Victorian house by the letting agent. Wearing a navy-blue suit and holding a clipboard, the letting agent reminded Bonnie of the driving instructor who had failed her when she was seventeen, and the woman from the human resources department at Bonnie's first place of work, which Bonnie had left at the end of a trial period, and the bank employee who had turned down her loan request, and someone else Bonnie was unable to recall. The letting agent shook Bonnie's hand and looked at her clipboard, and Bonnie braced herself for some sort of test.

'Mrs Falls?' said the letting agent.

'Miss,' said Bonnie. 'Ms,' she added, and the sound she made was like air escaping through a puncture, the sound of something slowly deflating.

'I'm sorry,' said the letting agent, making a note on her clipboard. 'Are we waiting for anyone else or it just you?'

'It's just me,' said Bonnie.

'That's fine,' said the letting agent. Scribbling again, she said something that Bonnie did not catch, and then, 'Single?'

'I'm sorry?' said Bonnie. She could imagine her mother having hired this woman—the navy-blue suit a disguise, the clipboard just a prop—to conduct an investigation into Bonnie's love life and come up with an answer, a solution. Bonnie

14

thought of her school's careers adviser biting the end of her pen and frowning. She thought of her mother saying, 'You're not a bad-looking girl, Bonnie. You just need to brighten yourself up. You just need to smile.' Bonnie had occasional dates with men she met online, but they rarely progressed to a second date, and never to a third. She was never, it seemed, quite anyone's type.

'Single tenancy?' said the letting agent.

'Yes,' said Bonnie.

The letting agent ticked a box on the paperwork on her clipboard, and Bonnie looked at the house. Its front—a flat, orange-bricked rectangle standing on its short side, with a pointy, orange-tiled roof on top—made her think of a gingerbread house, the clean frames like white icing around the square windows and the front door.

'There are two flats available in this property,' said the letting agent. 'An attic flat and a ground-floor flat. Did you want to see them both today?'

'No,' said Bonnie. 'Just the ground-floor flat.'

'All right,' said the letting agent. 'You can always change your mind. Let's go and see the downstairs flat first.'

Bonnie was led through a passageway between the house and its immediate neighbour, down a red-brick path like the one in the film of *The Wizard of Oz*, in which, at first, a red-brick road and a yellow-brick road spiralled together, like the pattern on a spinning top that Bonnie had lost in childhood. Dorothy took the yellow-brick road, while the red-brick road went off in another direction, and you never found out where it led. In the book, though, there was no option, no red-brick road. Also in the book, the yellow-brick road was interrupted in places by deep drops with sharp and jagged rocks at the bottom, which Bonnie did not remember seeing in the film. And what was only a dream in the film was, in the book, quite real.

The passageway led to the house's back door, and they entered the ground-floor flat through the kitchen, which had a three-foot-wide aisle down the middle and work surfaces on either side. The letting agent pointed out the fixtures and fittings, and any damage that she was aware of. 'It's all on the inventory,' she said, referring to her clipboard, which held a list of what was provided and what was damaged, with no division between the two: the kitchen contained a fridge and a missing drawer handle, a cooker and a missing vinyl floor tile.

A narrow bathroom extended from one end of the kitchen, and at the other end you walked into a long lounge barely touched by natural light, and beyond that was the bedroom. Living in this flat, thought Bonnie, would be like living in a series of corridors. The bedroom, at the front of the flat, looked directly onto the street and the bus stop outside.

In the bedroom's side wall, there was a door. 'What's behind this door?' asked Bonnie, reaching for the door handle, but the letting agent said that it led only to the other part of the house, the hallway that the front door opened into, and the stairs to the upper floors. Now that the house had been divided into flats, this door remained locked, she said, although Bonnie tried the handle anyway.

At the end of February, Bonnie moved into the flat on a six-month tenancy agreement. She had recently been turned down by a temp agency but she had two cleaning jobs. She was hoping to find something she liked better. She kept putting in applications but rarely got interviews; and when she did get an interview, she never got the job. For now, her parents were supplementing her rent. She could not afford to buy anything for the flat but it came partially furnished anyway; there was even an old television. And she brought some home comforts with her from her parents' house: she had a kettle that her mother had been about to throw out, and a small supply of tea bags to tide her over, and she had her books. She had more books than shelf space: on either side of the bookcase in the lounge, the books spread in piles across the floor, reaching towards the doors, towards the bedroom and the kitchen, as if they were trying to get out, to go out into the world. She did her best to make the flat feel like hers, putting her own bedding on the mattress, and placing her knickknacks around the lounge, though they looked a bit lost in that long, dim room. She moved them around a little.

In the kitchen, in a drawer, she found a memo, or a partial shopping list. It said, 'BUY WOTSITS'. Bonnie had not bought Wotsits for years. In a cupboard, she found dozens of hoarded newspapers, with items clipped out. She found a picture postcard, with a design from the 1930s, advertising Butlin's holiday camps in Skegness and Clacton-on-Sea; it said 'JOIN OUR HAPPY FAMILY'. She turned it over but the side the sender was supposed to write on was blank. At the back of a drawer in the bedroom, Bonnie found a new-ish pair of socks, which she kept, even though they were a bit small, a bit tight. They would be useful, she thought, in an emergency. In the under-stairs cupboard—which was in her part of the house even though the stairs themselves were not—she found a huge amount of stuff presumably left behind by a previous tenant: a cardboard box full of dusty baby blankets; a cooler; a camping stove; a table with folding legs, like a picnic table, or a wallpaper pasting table; a pair of Anglepoise lamps and a torch; a case of LPs but nothing to play them on; old coats and shoes. People lived with so much crap, she thought, peering into this cupboard whose back wall she could not even see. She shut the door. It was astonishing what people came across when they moved into old houses. She had read about people finding—in their attics and cellars—antiques, old masters, old letters and diaries, or they found guns and grenades, mummified squirrels and mice, birds and bats, cat bones and dog bones and human bones. Sometimes, they lived in these places for years with no idea that these things were there, just below their feet, just above their heads. But Bonnie had found nothing like that.

She had been in the flat for some weeks before she got around to investigating a lumpy bit of carpet in the middle of the lounge. Peeling back the thin, beige carpet—which had been cut to only approximately the right size and shape and laid like a rug, without gripper at the edges—Bonnie found, underneath it, an old paint-tin lid lying on the floorboards. Its crust of paint was the same colour as the lounge walls. The work that had been done to make this place seem habitable—the slapping on of magnolia and the snipping out of a rough bit of carpet—was somewhat superficial, giving the room a temporary feel, like a stage set.

So, thought Bonnie: no old masters, no grenades, no bones; just newspapers, socks, a paint-tin lid, and the contents of the deep and jam-packed cupboard under the stairs. And sometimes, through the walls or through the ceiling, from the other part of the house, came the sound of someone else's music or the smell of someone else's cooking; a familiar film score would make her tap her foot, or her mouth would start watering at the smell of home cooking coming from the upstairs flat; and when her bedroom was dark, she saw a sliver of light coming through underneath the locked door.

3

B ONNIE'S MORNING CLEANING job was at an amusement arcade on the high street. She walked there past an old house that had the ghost of an advert painted on its side wall, clinging faintly to the brickwork: *EAT* . . . She passed a chip shop and high-rise buildings and a car park from which a man had jumped, the son of someone her mother knew. She passed a church, with posters stapled to a board outside, saying 'GOD WILL SAVE YOU'. She passed the community centre on Waterside Close, with scalloped stone edging around the doorway, and happy cartoon characters stuck to the windows, or starting to come away. She might once have gone to the playgroup there; she had the vaguest sense of having been abandoned in that building. There was graffiti on the exterior walls that said things like 'HOPE' and 'BOOM!'

On the high street itself, she passed a pet shop in which she used to work. The pet shop had a resident parrot that sat on a perch and seemed to watch her, and every now and again it said, 'You stink!' The parrot surely did not mean her personally, and Bonnie was not even sure that parrots had a sense of smell, but still she would surreptitiously put her nose to her armpit and sniff, although she could not tell if what she could smell was just the hamsters in their cages, on their wheels. Either way, it had not been good for her self-esteem.

After keeping the pet shop job for longer than any other, she had got her current morning job in the amusement arcade, where she vacuumed the carpet tiles and cleaned the machines. She wiped the backlit buttons that said things like 'PRESS', 'PUSH', 'PUSH!', 'HOLD' and 'GO', buffing away the build-up of fingerprints made by the punters' fingertips pecking and pecking at the buttons, waiting for the payout. She polished the chrome-effect trim on the change machine as if it were a magic lamp.

Bonnie had a few hours free in the afternoon, before her second job. Usually, she went to the chip shop. The chips were wrapped in butcher paper, the sort that she had done her paintings on when she was still in infant school: pictures of her house and her garden, and her family holding hands; it was the sort of paper that her mother sometimes brought lamb chops home in. The chips in those days were wrapped in newspaper; Bonnie remembered sitting on a wall with a hot packet of greasy, salty chips on her bare thighs, the newspaper print coming off on her skin. *Lose weight*, said the ink on her legs, but backwards.

In the middle of town, there was a bench with a plaque on it: 'In loving memory of' someone or other. On the wooden slats, someone had written, in thick, black marker pen in two separate places, 'CUNT'. If the bench was free, Bonnie would sit there with her chips. The two pieces of graffiti were placed such that whichever side she sat on, the word 'CUNT' would remain visible beside her, like a label.

She watched the kids skateboarding and training to do parkour. Someone had said—some parkour expert—that thinking you are going to fail at something gives you a higher risk of doing just that. She wondered if that was true, and supposed she could test it, though not right now, in front of everyone; she would fall flat on her face.

Sometimes, after her chips, she went to the cinema. She might watch a film more than once during its run, as if she expected it to be different the second or third time. During these matinee showings, she was often the only person in the auditorium. In the dark, she ate her popcorn and lost herself in the film, something historical or futuristic, something set in another country or on another planet. It only took an hour or so, ninety minutes, for the world outside to become unreal. When she emerged, the familiar town would look strange, like a set, the oblivious shoppers like walk-ons. After horror films, she felt uneasy in broad daylight, and made an effort to avoid alleyways and underpasses and anywhere deserted; she felt compelled to glance behind her as she walked, although she tried hard not to look, to just keep walking, looking straight ahead. The film score remained in her ears and would come back to her at odd times throughout the day, for years.

The walk to her second job took her past an animal rescue centre, a cat sanctuary. When she got close, she could hear what might have been dozens of unwanted cats, a hundred cats, miaowing, or else she imagined that she could. What happened, she wondered, to the cats that could not find an owner, the ones that were just too old to be chosen? Some places had a 'no kill' policy; she did not know about this particular sanctuary. And presumably a lack of space meant that there were some cats that did not make it into the shelter in the first place. One day, instead of walking past, she would go in. If she went in, she would want to take a cat home; if she chose one, she would want to choose three or four; she would want to take them all, every last one. She would be the kind of woman who was always mocked, a woman with a houseful of rescue cats, except that she did not have a house, and was not allowed pets in the flat.

At the end of the afternoon, Monday to Friday, Bonnie cleaned at a pharmaceutical research and development laboratory, which was in the middle of a normal street of old, red-brick terraced houses, whose tiles were slipping and whose chimneys and garden walls were crumbling and toppling—you could imagine the whole street falling to pieces in a storm—but the pharmaceutical complex was new; it was squat and sturdy.

She shared her shift at the Lab with a woman called Chi. The supervisor, Mr Carr, called her Chichi, which Chi found infuriating. This only encouraged him.

On days when Bonnie did not arrive late, she and Chi would sit together in the staff room before starting their shift, and Bonnie would get something out of the vending machine—a packet of crisps or sweets or a chocolate bar. Sometimes, there was a competition running, and Bonnie would have a chance of winning something: 'WIN £500 CASH' said the shiny packets. At least one company had apparently hidden tracking devices in certain products, in the wrappers of half a dozen bars of chocolate, so that they could track you down and leap out and give you a briefcase full of cash, ten thousand pounds. Or she could win a holiday, or a car: 'WIN INSTANTLY' said the products, from behind the toughened glass of the vending machine, and she did try.

'Win, win, win,' she whispered to a brand-new packet of sweets.

'What was that?' asked Chi. 'What did you say?'

'You can win a prize,' said Bonnie, 'if you've got the lucky packet.'

'But saying "win, win, win" won't make a difference,' said Chi. 'You've either got the winning packet or you haven't.'

'I always say it,' replied Bonnie.

'And have you ever won?' asked Chi.

'It worked the very first time I tried it.'

'Does it work every time?'

'I don't think it's worked since then,' said Bonnie, 'but what if one time I *would* have won if I'd said it, but then I didn't say it and so I lost?'

Chi leaned towards the packet of sweets and said, 'Lose, lose, lose.'

Bonnie winced. 'What did you do that for?' she complained, looking anxiously at the little packet.

'It makes no difference,' said Chi. 'You have no control over whether you win or lose. You know that, don't you?'

Bonnie did not reply. She was busy looking inside the packet to see if she had won, but she had not.

From five to seven o'clock, Bonnie mopped the long corridors in the main building. The corridors led past sets of double doors: big, white doors with no windows in them. She wondered what was behind these blank doors, what grim experiments might be taking place. She thought about monkey experiments, like Dr Harlow's monkeys: newborns taken from their mothers and made to choose between a bare-wire, milk-giving 'mother' and a cloth-covered, milkless 'mother'. This was not that sort of laboratory, of course, but still, when she saw the secretive double doors, she thought of those unhappy monkeys clinging to their make-believe mothers. Or else she thought of dogs being made to smoke cigarettes, and rabbits having chemicals dripped into their unblinking eyes. There were some things that the scientists were not allowed to do these days, but she was not sure exactly what, quite where the line had been drawn.

Or perhaps it was just a store room, a stationery cupboard, full of letterhead and window envelopes, spare pens and pencils, toner cartridges and boxes of paperclips so that they need never run out, so that the paperwork could always be completed.

Chi, who cleaned a different section of the complex, disliked the job even more than Bonnie did. She had once said to Bonnie, 'I don't like what they do here,' and Bonnie had nodded. 'I think we should leave,' Chi had added, but then Mr Carr had appeared on the scene, and Bonnie had opened her mouth and started to say that she was not sure that she could leave, that she needed the work, the money, that it could be worse, but Chi picked up her bucket and walked away, and Bonnie had to go to her first long corridor and start work.

At the end of the shift, Bonnie and Chi would go back to the staff room to collect their belongings, and Mr Carr would be there too, to make sure that they were not sneaking off early or stealing anything. He would check their pockets and their bags, whose contents he sometimes emptied out onto the tabletop, and when they left, he would say, 'I'm watching you.'

Sometimes, at night, after walking back to the flat on Slash Lane—where the street lamps flickered and sometimes went off—Bonnie had trouble sleeping.

In the night, she found herself at her bedroom window, whose curtains did not meet in the middle. Seeing a star, one very bright star in the otherwise empty sky, she thought to herself, *There's the North Star*. She did not know much about what was out there but she thought she knew that: she was looking at the North Star, and the North Star was a constant, a guiding light. She whispered to it:

> *Star light, star bright,*
> *The first star I see tonight . . .*

Or, she thought, was she wrong about that? Did the role of North Star switch from one star to another as everything moved around in the sky? And then she saw that this bright star she was looking at was moving even as she watched it, the dot of light sliding from one side of the window frame to the other, and she thought of those old films where people are pretending to be driving along while the background scrolls past, to give the impression that the people themselves are moving.

The light in the sky was just an aeroplane. Perhaps someone was going on holiday, in the middle of the night.

> *Pressed against the windowpane,*
> *Wishing on an aeroplane.*

Awake in the early hours, she put on her dressing gown and pottered. She had continued to find all sorts of unexpected things secreted about the place. In the cupboard under the stairs, she discovered three artificial Christmas trees, and a collection of road signs—red-bordered triangles—and traffic cones that ought to have been around holes in the road. On top of the wardrobe in the bedroom, she found a suitcase full of dressing-up clothes: Halloween costumes—a witch, a devil, a Frankenstein mask, or rather Dr Frankenstein's monster—

and a clown costume, or perhaps the clown was also a Hallow-een outfit. And in the drawer of the old Mission desk in the lounge, she found a little origami figure that made her think of a fat, flightless bird like a chicken, or a dodo. She did not know whether these things ought to be returned to someone or whether they were hers now, but she did not want all these things: the fake trees, the costumes, the warning signs. She would mention it to the letting agent, but it did not bother her too much for the time being. In university accommodation, she had put up for the best part of a year with a mattress whose springs poked through, stabbing into her flesh as she slept.

Or sometimes, when she could not sleep, she would go to the all-night garage and buy something. On her birthday, she bought a packet of Love Hearts that said 'CRAZY' and 'DREAM ON'.

Or else she would open up her laptop and try to write, although mostly she ended up on the Internet. It just hap-pened: one moment, she would be looking at an opening paragraph, trying to bring something to mind, her fingers hov-ering over the keyboard, and the next moment she would have clicked and she would find herself online, window-shopping; she would try not to let the cursor—which turned into a little hand with its index finger extended, as if, like a child, it wanted to touch everything—stray towards the targeted advertising, the flashing buttons that said 'SHOP NOW', 'BUY NOW', and when she did, she worried about the people who were out there waiting to phish her. She pictured them as if they were just beyond the screen, waiting for her to make a move. One day, she would click on some link without realising what it was and then her cursor would start moving around on the screen, with a life of its own, and that would be it, they would be in.

4

ONE SATURDAY MORNING, Bonnie was woken by the sound of someone knocking at the back door. She lay in bed for a moment, wondering whether she could ignore it, but the knocking persisted and in the end Bonnie put on her dressing gown and went to see who it was.

The doors at the front and back of her parents' house were solid, but this door had a small pane of glass, like an A4 sheet of graph paper, and through it Bonnie could see a woman, waiting. Something about this made Bonnie feel nervous. It was the graph-paper glass, she thought, which made her think of tests that she was unlikely to pass.

Bonnie opened the door. The woman standing on her doormat—a tall woman wearing a sheepskin coat—looked at Bonnie with a degree of interest that made Bonnie feel uneasy, and she touched the front of her dressing gown to check that it was securely fastened. The woman's big, bright eyes made Bonnie feel like Little Red Riding Hood being looked at by the wolf. The woman smiled.

'Can I help you?' asked Bonnie.

'I'm Sylvia Slythe,' said the woman, holding out a long-fingered, long-nailed hand. 'I'm your landlady, dear. I live upstairs.'

'Oh,' said Bonnie, taking a sideways glance at the washing-up that she had not yet done, the dirty pots and pans and tins spread over the counters. She had not been expecting visitors. The landlady, still smiling, moved her shiny shoe towards the threshold, and Bonnie took a step backwards, barefoot on the sticky lino. The landlady came into the kitchen.

'Would you like a cup of tea, Mrs Slythe?' asked Bonnie.

'Call me Sylvia,' she said.

'Sylvia,' said Bonnie.

'Thank you, dear, that would be lovely.'

'How do you take it?' asked Bonnie, opening the fridge.

'White with two sugars, please,' said Sylvia.

'Oh,' said Bonnie, peering into the fridge. 'I'm out of milk.'

'Never mind,' said Sylvia. 'We can have it black.'

'I haven't got any sugar, either,' said Bonnie, looking inside the empty pot that had 'SUGAR' written optimistically on the side.

Sylvia smiled. 'Whatever you can manage is fine,' she said.

Bonnie carried their mugs of black, unsweetened tea through to the lounge, where she offered Sylvia a seat on the sofa, although it did occur to Bonnie that all the seats in the house were really her landlady's anyway. Sylvia removed her sheepskin coat, underneath which she was wearing a suit jacket, which she left on. It was a cold spring day and just as cold inside the house as out. Sylvia's jacket matched her blue skirt, attached to the belt loop of which was a bunch of keys, which made her look a bit like a jailer, but more ladylike. Sylvia smoothed her skirt beneath her as she sat down.

Bonnie handed Sylvia the bigger mug, which had 'I'M A MUG!' printed on the side. It was one of Bonnie's favourites but it looked wrong, she thought, in Sylvia's elegant hands.

Sylvia accepted her tea with a smile and said, 'I just came to see how you were getting on.'

'Fine,' said Bonnie. 'Absolutely fine.'

'Are you still unpacking?' asked Sylvia, nodding towards one corner of the room, in which were piled some of the cases and boxes that Bonnie had found in the flat and which she had never got around to mentioning to the letting agent. 'Or were you thinking of moving out already?'

'Oh,' said Bonnie. 'None of that's mine. I just found it here.'

In another corner were the three artificial Christmas trees. It looked as if a dinky little fairy tale forest were sprouting through the floorboards, like something dreamt up by the Brothers Grimm.

Along the wall in between the two corners were all the traffic cones and red-triangle road signs. Some of the signs were folded, leaning, with their backs to the wall, and some of them were erect. They looked as if they had been put there to warn of some danger in the flat: a lump in the carpet that someone might trip over, or a hole in the ground into which someone might stumble.

The whole thing looked like an art installation, something that a person might stand in front of at an end-of-year show, trying to see some meaning or message in it.

'I don't know where it all came from,' said Bonnie. 'I didn't know what to do with it.'

'There was a student living here before you,' said Sylvia. 'But he wasn't here for long. I had no idea he'd hoarded all those signs.' With an expansive sweep of her hand, like someone on a game show indicating what could be won, or what had not been won, she said, 'Consider it gone.'

Bonnie bent her head to her mug of black tea, burning her lips and the inside of her mouth.

'Do sit down,' said Sylvia. Bonnie adjusted her dressing gown and sat down next to her landlady. 'You have a familiar name,' said Sylvia. 'Bonnie Falls,' she added, as if Bonnie might not know it. Bonnie had always been disconcerted by the thought of strangers holding her details in their files, and Sylvia was one of them.

'Do I?' she asked.

'May I ask your mother's name?' enquired Sylvia, and Bonnie told Sylvia her mother's maiden name, which appeared only briefly on the family tree that Bonnie had seen, on which all the women's branches were short, their names disappearing, while what her father called 'the main, true line' went back for generations. He was not interested in 'the peripheral lines,' the female lines, on which the names changed every generation, as if the women themselves were fickle and flighty. Although, in fact, the 'Falls' line was not entirely stable either: from the top to the bottom of the tree, the name changed from Faill to Fall to Falls.

'No,' said Sylvia, 'not her maiden name. What's your mother's first name?'

'Oh,' said Bonnie. 'Pearl. Why?' Her landlady was not filling in forms.

'Pearl,' echoed Sylvia. 'Good.' She grinned, displaying large teeth in a wide mouth. 'I think I knew her,' she said. 'And you, as well, when you were little.' She tested her tea and then asked how Bonnie's mother was.

'She's fine,' said Bonnie.

'Is she?' said Sylvia, and Bonnie thought she seemed surprised, and slightly disappointed. 'Tell me about her,' said

Sylvia, so Bonnie talked about her mother's career and her various committees and achievements, and Sylvia seemed increasingly disheartened. Bonnie mentioned her mother's success in amateur skiing competitions; she had just flown out to compete in another one. Her mother was generally adventurous. She had taken an infant-school-aged Bonnie to Japan, where they had climbed Mount Tenjo. There was a photograph of the two of them on their way up the mountain path. The label in the album said: *On Mount Tenjo, with Mount Fuji in the background.* Mount Fuji was not visible in the photograph, but Bonnie recalled how, while they stood there on the mountain path, the dense, white cloud beyond the trees had shifted, revealing, in the vast skyscape, a sliver of something huge, the dark edge of Mount Fuji emerging like a soft pencil line drawn on the blank sky. Then the cloud had moved again, obscuring the mountain, and the camera's shutter had clicked. She remembered, as well, being told about the giant catfish that slept beneath Tokyo Bay. Its wriggling caused Tokyo's daily tremors, and one day, after decades of sleeping, it would wake and cause a major earthquake. 'But it's only a story,' her mother had added. Bonnie, though, had felt the tremors, which shuddered through her in the night.

'I'm not like my mother at all,' said Bonnie to Sylvia.

'Are you not?'

'No. I can't ski, and I don't fly. I avoid heights.' She had flown to Japan; she'd had no problem with it then. When, more recently, Bonnie's problems had become apparent, her mother had suggested medication, so that she would be able to get on with her life, to fly and so on. Bonnie, though, whilst afraid of being up high, was even more wary of being up high and feeling no fear.

'And I didn't get on very well at school,' added Bonnie.

'Don't mumble,' said Sylvia.

'At school, my reports tended to say things like I was going nowhere, which I suppose is proving to be true,' said Bonnie. 'At secondary school I failed a lot of my exams. So I don't have the sort of career my mum would like me to have.'

'You failed your exams?' said Sylvia, leaning forward in a way that seemed sympathetic.

'A lot of them,' said Bonnie. She mentioned that she had recently been having another go at learning French, her attempts at school having been so dismal, and that her mother had bought her audio lessons and had suggested listening to the course at night—'You'll learn it in your sleep,' her mother had said—but Bonnie was wary of having it dripped into her unconscious self like that. She would be like the child in *Brave New World* who suddenly knew that *The-Nile-is-the-longest-river-in-Africa* but not what that meant.

'I would be interested to know,' said Sylvia, 'if you have any success with that method.'

'I find it very difficult to get the language to stick in my brain,' said Bonnie, hammering at her skull with her fingertips.

'The younger you are, the easier it is,' said Sylvia. 'You learn your first language effortlessly, just picking it up from the people around you and assimilating it.' She mentioned the language deprivation experiments that had been conducted on children by pharaohs and emperors and kings throughout the ages, experiments designed to see what language the children would grow up to speak without any intervention. 'I do find it interesting,' said Sylvia, 'this question of the extent to which language is an internal impulse or an external knowledge to be acquired. It's unfortunate,' she added, 'that these language experiments also tended to necessitate social deprivation, sometimes almost complete isolation. I believe the experiments led to some deaths.'

'That's terrible,' said Bonnie. 'No one would dream of doing that these days. No one would allow it to happen.'

'It seems unlikely, doesn't it?' said Sylvia.

Bonnie told Sylvia about going to university but finding it hard and failing to complete her degree.

'At what point did you leave your course?' asked Sylvia.

'In the final year,' said Bonnie. 'I've still got all the notes I made for my dissertation, but I never actually wrote it.'

Bonnie told Sylvia about the job she had taken after dropping out of university, her trial period, and how it had not really worked out. She told her about some things she had tried since, which had failed, including the temp agency that had not wanted her. 'I have a couple of cleaning jobs,' she said. 'My parents help me with the rent.'

'And what would you *like* to be doing?' asked Sylvia.

'Oh, I don't really know,' said Bonnie, glancing at the desk across the room, on top of which sat a laptop, which was closed, and a printer.

'Don't mumble,' said Sylvia, but she followed Bonnie's gaze. Bonnie reminded herself of a character in a book she had read, in which a woman, when asked about some wanted rogue she might be harbouring, denied that she had seen him but at the same time glanced at the scullery door that hid him. Bonnie looked away.

Sylvia regarded her for a moment, as if considering something. 'When you took this flat,' she said, 'were you aware that the top flat—the loft conversion—was also vacant?' She pointed to the ceiling. 'It has a good view.'

'Yes,' said Bonnie, 'but I prefer to live on the ground floor.'

Sylvia looked at her with interest. 'And why is that?' she asked.

'When I was a kid,' said Bonnie, 'I started sleepwalking. I'd wake up and find myself standing at a window, like I was looking out, although I wasn't really seeing, I suppose. But one time, the window was open, and Mum found me halfway out of it. She had to keep the windows locked and hide the keys.'

Bonnie reached for a pack of cigarettes that was lying on the arm of the sofa. She opened it and offered a cigarette to Sylvia, who declined. 'But I would accept another cup of tea,' she said, 'if you don't mind.'

'Of course,' said Bonnie, standing up, fixing the belt of her dressing gown, and taking the mugs back into the kitchen. While she waited for the kettle to boil again, she smoked her cigarette; there was no smoke alarm in the kitchen ceiling. Looking out into the backyard, she saw that it had started raining. She could not see the rain itself falling or landing; no drops were being blown against the window; but, in a waterlogged pothole outside the back door, in the puddle left behind by the previous day's rainfall, she could see the little ripples that the rain made on the surface of the water, the tiny disturbances radiating outwards.

When Bonnie returned to the lounge with the two mugs of black tea, she found Sylvia standing over by the desk, reading. 'Oh,' said Bonnie, putting down the mugs. There was no coffee table, so she placed the mugs on the carpet and went over to the desk, where Sylvia was looking at the printout of the Seatown story. 'Did I leave that out?'

'You're a writer?' said Sylvia.

'Not really,' said Bonnie.

'But this is a story you've written?'

Bonnie took the story out of Sylvia's hands. 'It is a story I *tried* to write,' she said. 'It's only the beginning, but I print everything out in case the laptop fails, which happened once.' One moment, she had been staring at a Word document, with her fingers poised over the keys, and the next moment the screen had gone blue and an emoticon was looking at her sadly, and then the screen went black. 'It's bound to happen again. I keep the printouts in case I ever want to go back to them, although I never do.'

Bonnie saw all sorts of advice for would-be writers: 'Write the moment you wake up, when you're in a hypnagogic state and can access your subconscious.' What Bonnie wrote sitting up in bed in the morning, what she netted from her subconscious always seemed like so much hogwash. Or else she made notes as she was falling asleep, and then, when she looked at them again days or weeks or months later, could not understand what on earth it all meant. 'Walk around in your fictional world as if it were the set of a soap opera; enter its buildings and approach its inhabitants.' Bonnie did not see how this could be done. She read that fictional characters have free will, but she did not see how this was possible. 'There is inspiration everywhere—you just need to train yourself to notice it.' Perhaps she needed something like the pair of special glasses that John Nada discovered in *They Live*, which enabled a person to see something more, a hidden world beneath the manifest one; although when John Nada looked beneath the surface, what he saw was 'SLEEP', 'STAY ASLEEP', 'OBEY'.

'You're not a writer,' said Sylvia, 'unless you're writing.'

Bonnie put the Seatown story back inside the desk's wide drawer, on a little pile of other abandoned openings. At the same time, Sylvia was reaching in, touching some of the pristine stationery that Bonnie had in there.

'You've got some beautiful notebooks in here,' said Sylvia. 'This one's covered in genuine calfskin,' she noted, admiring the finish.

'My mum gave me that one,' said Bonnie.

Her mother had said, 'Now you'll look like a writer,' as if that were the point, as if a pair of wing-tipped spectacles and a purple scarf were all Bonnie needed, as well as all the cats. Some people did wear special outfits in order to write, or else they used a lucky pen, but Bonnie did not have one of those.

'I thought the notebooks might help,' said Bonnie, 'but I can't write in them, they're too nice. I'm bound to spoil them.' She shut the drawer and returned to the sofa, where she gulped down her tea like a victim recovering from shock, except that her tea was not sweet.

Sylvia stayed by the desk. 'This story you were trying to write,' she said, 'is about a girl who is living in an attic room, and who dreams about jumping out of the window.'

'Dreamt,' said Bonnie, 'once, when she was little.'

'All right,' said Sylvia, '*dreamt* of jumping out of a window, and then moved into an attic room. And how will your story end?'

'I don't know,' said Bonnie.

'You've no idea how your story ends?'

'No.'

'But if you write it,' said Sylvia, 'you'll find out.'

'If I wrote it I would,' said Bonnie, 'yes.'

'What does it say on the piece of paper that's appeared under the door?' asked Sylvia.

'I don't know,' said Bonnie.

'But it does say something,' said Sylvia, 'doesn't it?'

'I'm not sure,' said Bonnie. 'I think so.'

'But Bonnie can't quite see it.'

'Susan,' said Bonnie. 'Susan can't see it.'

'Yes, of course,' said Sylvia. 'Susan.'

'It makes me think of the messages that appeared each morning on Cézanne's doormat,' said Bonnie, 'when he was in Aix, nearing death.'

'What did those messages say?' asked Sylvia.

'They told him to leave town,' said Bonnie.

'Who put those messages through his door?'

'His neighbours, I think,' said Bonnie.

'And who posted this message under Susan's door?'

'I don't know.'

'The landlady, presumably,' Sylvia suggested.

'I'm not sure who else it could be,' agreed Bonnie.

'Well, it's up to you, is it not?' said Sylvia. 'You are the writer. You decide whether and why your character does something. You must know.'

'I'm sure I should know,' said Bonnie, 'but I don't.'

'So you are not really in control of your own story?'

'I'm not sure I am,' said Bonnie.

'When did you write this?' asked Sylvia.

Bonnie sighed. 'I started writing it in the winter, before moving in here, but, you know, I feel like I've been writing it for years, like every time I write anything it's really the same thing I'm writing about.'

'But you still don't know how it should end?'

'No. I've given up with it anyway. I don't really know what the story's about.'

'It's about failure,' said Sylvia, 'and fear.'

'Oh,' said Bonnie. 'Is it?'

Sylvia turned to the bookcase beside the desk. 'You have a lot of self-help books,' she said.

'My mum gave them to me,' said Bonnie. She watched as Sylvia ran her index finger along the spines: *Making the Most of Yourself, How to Start a Conversation and Make Friends, How to Be Your Own Best Friend, Embracing Your Inner Critic*. Here and there Sylvia paused, like a doctor preparing to press down on bared skin so as to find out where the pain was: *Does it hurt here? What about here?* 'Fail,' said Sylvia, '*Fail Again, Fail Better.*' She took out the book she was looking at. 'So,' she said, nodding to the words on the cover. 'Can you lean into the unknown?'

Bonnie shrugged.

Sylvia took down another book, showing Bonnie the cover as if she might not have seen her own books before. '*TRY AGAIN,*' she read. '*FAIL AGAIN. FAIL BETTER.*' She slid the book back into place. 'Have you read them all?' she asked.

'Yes,' said Bonnie. 'But not necessarily all the way through.'

'Susan,' said Sylvia. 'Susan is your middle name, isn't it?'

'Yes,' said Bonnie, 'it is.' She did not recall putting this detail down on any paperwork when she had taken the flat, but then she remembered that Sylvia had known her mother, and herself, apparently.

'You look like her,' said Sylvia, eyeing Bonnie.

'Like my mum?' asked Bonnie.

'No,' said Sylvia. 'She was blond, I think. Slim and very well turned out. No. I mean Susan. You have her short, brown hair, though not her legs.'

Bonnie tugged the hem of her dressing gown over her bared, broad knees.

'You could have given your character any name you wanted to,' said Sylvia.

'What's wrong with Susan?' asked Bonnie. 'It's just a name.'

'Names are important,' said Sylvia. 'Judy Garland was not Frances Ethel Gumm. Cary Grant was not Archibald Leach. Marilyn Monroe could not remain a Norma.'

'They were still the same people, though,' said Bonnie, 'whatever they were called.' Nonetheless, she wondered whether her parents ever felt that they had chosen the wrong name for her, whether it had been optimistic, like when she had given the name Lucky to a fairground goldfish that turned out to be diseased.

'You work in an amusement arcade, don't you?' said Sylvia. 'Like the one in your story, in which Susan is offered a job?'

'Yes,' said Bonnie, 'but I don't work in a change booth, which is the job Susan's offered, and anyway, Susan never actually works there.'

'Did you have the dream Susan has about jumping out of your bedroom window?' asked Sylvia.

'I'm not Susan,' said Bonnie.

'No,' said Sylvia, 'of course not.' She smiled. 'Our dreams, according to Freud, are wish-fulfilments. What do you dream about, Bonnie?'

'I rarely remember my dreams,' said Bonnie.

'You're more likely to remember what the dream was about if you wake up in the middle of it,' said Sylvia. 'Perhaps you sleep very soundly.'

'But if you woke up in the middle of it,' said Bonnie, 'you would never know how it ended.'

'Dreams rarely have proper endings,' said Sylvia. 'They just move on or suddenly stop, like life.' She sat down next to Bonnie again and sipped her tea. 'So you've written other things?' she asked.

'I haven't really finished anything,' said Bonnie. 'Sometimes things seem like they're going fine but then they just start going wrong.'

'I would very much like to see your other stories,' said Sylvia, 'even if they aren't finished, and even if they are no good.'

'Oh, no,' said Bonnie. 'I'd rather not. I don't—' But Sylvia had begun to cough, her shoulders hunching, her hand brought up to her chest.

When the cough subsided, Sylvia said, 'Do excuse me. It's just a tickle. Do you think I could have a glass of water?'

'Of course,' said Bonnie, getting to her feet. She went to the kitchen and stayed there for a minute, hoping that the unseen germs would disperse in her absence. Or perhaps they were instead filling the room, multiplying.

When she returned to the lounge, Sylvia was on her feet, collecting up her things.

'I'm going to get going,' said Sylvia, pausing to accept the mug of water that Bonnie was passing to her, handing it back when she had taken a sip. 'Thank you so much,' she said. Indicating the things that were piled up in the corners of the room, she added, 'I'll send someone round to pick all this up.'

Bonnie walked Sylvia to the back door, and when they got there she thought to ask, 'How did you know my mother?'

'Oh, I knew her years ago,' said Sylvia. 'You were only little.' She stepped outside and then turned back. 'Bonnie,' she said, musing. 'It sounds like such a happy name, but the only Bonnies I can think of are Bonnie Parker of Bonnie and

Clyde, who was killed of course, and so young, and that song: *My Bonnie lies over the ocean, my Bonnie lies over the sea.*' She smiled then, said goodbye and walked away, disappearing into the passageway, her footsteps loud and echoing at first, and then fading. Bonnie closed the door.

She washed up the mugs and left them draining. What a nice lady, she thought; they had got on like a house on fire. She thought over what Sylvia had said, about her story, and her books, and her dreams, and her name, and about knowing her mother. And there was something else, she thought, that she felt she was trying to remember, but it escaped her, and in the end she boiled the kettle again and turned on the telly. In between programmes, during the advert breaks when she went to the kitchen for Wotsits, and when she got into bed that night, the words of that song were in her head: *Bring back, bring back, oh bring back my Bonnie to me.*

5

B ONNIE FALLS HAS tried to write, but has failed to finish,
at least half a dozen short stories, including her most
recent "Seatown" story. Her habit of leaving her work incom-
plete reminds me of the Egyptians leaving a gap in their
hieroglyphs of serpents, which they did, apparently, because
completing the hieroglyph risked bringing the serpent to life.

All of Bonnie's unfinished stories have been printed out and
kept together in the same place: in the drawer of my grandmother's old Mission desk. This desk used to stand in the hallway of
the house in which I grew up, and in its single, wide drawer my
grandmother kept all her personal paperwork. I was told, when
I was little: "Sylvia, you must not touch this desk. It is out of
bounds." Despite this caution, or perhaps because of it, I did,
quite compulsively, touch the Mission desk. Even when I was
really only walking past it, my arm would levitate and, before
I knew it, my fingers were touching the legs or the front of the
drawer. I could not help it. I was especially forbidden to open
the drawer, but it had no lock. The desk is now in my possession
anyway. It is in my house, in the ground-floor flat.

All these unfinished stories of Bonnie's are set by the
sea, and one must ask: why this obsession with the sea? She
does not live there, although she could. When considering

this question, one ought to take into account the fact that in each of Bonnie's stories—as well as in many of the novels on her bookshelves—the sea is a metaphor for death. Correspondingly, to be at the seaside is to be at the edge of death. The seashore is a threshold. This, in fact, seems to have been the focus of Bonnie's unfinished dissertation, which she had been sketching out before abandoning her university course. I have had the opportunity of seeing the pages of notes made in preparation for this major piece of work, which was never completed, and I have endeavoured to put them into some sort of order here.

Bonnie's notes refer to the ancient seashore being "haunted by the possibility of a monster bursting forth", a monster that might represent an invader, or the Black Death, or there might be actual monsters, "nightmarish creatures born out of black waters" (Corbin, *The Lure of the Sea: The Discovery of the Seaside in the Western World 1750–1840*). The monsters might even have names, like Leviathan or the Kraken, or they might be unnamed, like the inhuman sea creatures of Innsmouth—"They were mostly shiny and slippery, but the ridges of their backs were scaly. Their forms vaguely suggested the anthropoid, while their heads were the heads of fish, with prodigious bulging eyes that never closed" (Lovecraft, *The Shadow Over Innsmouth*)—or like the shark in *Jaws* (for the modern-day seashore remains equally haunted, it seems, by the possibility of a monster bursting forth). The sea, writes Bonnie, is the domain of the Under Toad, a misunderstanding of the word "undertow", an unseen danger: "lurking offshore, waiting to suck him under and drag him out to sea. The terrible Under Toad . . . Would it ever surface?" The reek of toad, the Under Toad's "swampy smell", is the reek of death (Irving, *The World According to Garp*). The monster might even be seen, might indeed burst forth: "*I saw a monster rising from the waves* . . . However: it is possible, perhaps plausible, to conjecture that the sea monster which I 'saw' was a hallucination" (Murdoch, *The Sea, The Sea*). In Bonnie's books, the sea itself has waves "like huge mouths snapping at the empty air, waiting for us" (Olmi, *Beside the Sea*). The sea is something that devours. The children are "made uneasy by this waveless, unstoppable tide, the sinister, calm way it kept coming on", and so they should be: "whatever cliffs there may once have been the sea had long ago eroded" (Banville, *The Sea*).

The sea represents the dimmer regions of the subconscious, inhabited by dreams and nightmares—"She thought: people slip off the shores of the real world, back into dreams" (Swift, "Learning to Swim")—and by madness: the ocean, "that unruly dark side of the world which was an abode of monsters stirred up by diabolical powers, emerges as one of the persistent figures of madness" (Corbin, *The Lure of the Sea*). To be in "the world under the sea", "at the bottom of the ocean", is to be in a "dead" mood, a trance-like state (Hamilton, *Hangover Square*). The philosophers Kant and Schopenhauer draw a parallel between dreaming and madness: Kant writes that, "The madman is a waking dreamer", and Schopenhauer calls dreams a brief madness and madness a long dream (Freud, *The Interpretation of Dreams*).

The sea, writes Bonnie, was believed to produce unhealthy emanations at the shore, "bad air", which might be attributed to the seaweed, the debris, "the excreta from the abyss", which accumulated on the sand (Corbin, *The Lure of the Sea*). And/or it might be explained by the sea being "a freezing great floating graveyard", so that taking a lilo into the shallows is akin to playing at the edge of an ancient Indian burial ground. The sea looks "like a torrent of mud", and being on the beach is like "being in a cardboard box", which suggests a makeshift coffin, ready for burial (Olmi, *Beside the Sea*).

The narratives themselves, notes Bonnie, have an untethered quality: "Later that day, the day the Graces came, or the following one, or the one following that, I saw the black car again" (Banville, *The Sea*). The narratives shift suddenly and easily from one time frame to another, or from one point of view to another. Or there are commas where one might expect full stops, and a lack of speech marks, giving a sense of fluidity, a lack of boundaries, one "sentence" washing into the next: "Kevin and Stanley were clean, they were getting ready for the night, as they said, yes, they often said I'm getting ready for the night, it's nice, getting yourself all sorted for the night, they never say I'm getting ready for the day, because daytime doesn't really warrant it, you've got to do it so you do, that's all, but at night there's a sort of preparation, like before a journey" (Olmi, *Beside the Sea*).

The "irresistible awakening of a collective desire for the shore" that arose around 1750 sounds to me like mass hypnosis. "Cure-takers began rushing toward the sea-shore . . . Along the desolate shore, the pleasant song of birds gives way to the sea-gull's harsh cry." The cure-takers' sea-bathing "was part of the aesthetics of the sublime: it involved facing the violent water, but without risk, enjoying the pretence that one could be swept under, and being struck by the full force of the waves, but without losing one's footing". My first thought, when I read these notes of Bonnie's, was that there *is* a risk, one *could* lose one's footing and be swept under, and that this activity must involve flirtation with a death wish. But it turns out that the female cure-taker had a supervisor: "The 'bathers' would plunge female patients into the water just as the wave broke, taking care to hold their heads down so as to increase the impression of suffocation." It sounds brutal, but the end result is that the fey young women become invigorated. The sea is bracing, if also dispassionately vicious. There is a note about exorcism, and when I first read it I thought that what was being referred to was the submersion of people so that they would be purified by the sea. In fact, it means sailors immersing relics into the water in order to purify the demonic sea. But it made me think of the bathers, the supervisors pushing the women's heads under the water, trying to force some change in them. "At the seaside, sheltered by the therapeutic alibi, a new world of sensations was growing out of the mixed pain and pleasure of sudden immersion . . . The sea-shore offered a stage on which, more than anywhere else, the actual spectacle of the confrontation between air, water, and land contributed to fostering daydreams about merging with the elemental forces and fantasies of being swallowed up" (Corbin, *The Lure of the Sea*).

In each of these novels and novellas, Bonnie recognises the compelling power of the sea's "siren's song" (Banville, *The Sea*). The sea, she suggests, is where the characters belong, where they want to be. A mother tells her child that the sea is "just saying how glad it is to see you, it's really missed you!" (Olmi, *Beside the Sea*). Far out at sea in his skiff, a fisherman thinks to himself, "I wish I was the fish . . . I would rather be that beast down there in the darkness of the sea" (Hemingway, *The Old Man and the Sea*). A student, and his cousin who is in the "madhouse", "shall swim out to that brooding reef in the sea and dive down through black abysses" (Lovecraft, *The Shadow Over Innsmouth*). The seashore represents a powerful "invitation to undertake a journey from which no one returns" (Corbin, *The Lure of the Sea*). Bonnie has written in the margin of her notes: "It is like the Land of Oz, which is surrounded by desert, and once you are there, it is almost impossible to leave."

Bonnie sees inevitability in the deaths in these seaside narratives. Even the train, she says, that George Harvey Bone is travelling on seems to sense this: "Approaching Brighton in the darkness, the train slowed down, hesitated, seemed to be feeling its way before risking itself in a dangerous area" (Hamilton, *Hangover Square*). The characters that come to the coast, feels Bonnie, are just as surely coming to their end, one way or another. After coming on holiday to a coastal city, Lise "will be found tomorrow morning dead". While Lise is devising her own murder, the maid at the hotel "inquires amiably if Madam is going to the beach" (Spark, *The Driver's Seat*). Meursault thinks that he might not, after all, commit murder, "But the whole beach, pulsing with heat, was pressing on my back" (Camus, *The Outsider*). He is condemned to death. Characters walk steadily into the water: "Then calmly they stood up and waded into the sea, the water smooth as oil hardly breaking around them, and leaned forward in unison and swam out slowly . . . out, and out" (Banville, *The Sea*), or they plunge from the eroding cliffs into the sea that is waiting below: "And if death had come her way it was no more than she had asked for. She had gone to meet him halfway" (Drabble, *The Witch of Exmoor*).

The above, then, is what Bonnie has picked out of her source material. Out of all that text, all that imagery, this is what she has homed in on, this is how she sees. It is like how a dog sees: a monochrome wash and then a vivid patch of blue, someone's blue jumper picked out, like the little girl's red coat in *Schindler's List*. This is Bonnie's sea: *Here be monsters*. While Bonnie herself lives in the Midlands, about as far away from the coast as she could be, it is to the shore of this sea that Bonnie keeps sending the characters in the stories that she writes.

6

N$^{\text{O ONE CAME}}$ to take away all the stuff that had been left behind in Bonnie's flat. She had grown used, though, to living with the cases and boxes that made it look as if she had not quite made up her mind about staying, and she hardly noticed the traffic cones and the signs, except for when she tripped over them in the dark. She began to think that if this stuff was not there, in the corners of the lounge, the room might feel oddly empty. She thought of those spaces in which homeowners sometimes discovered strangers living, homeless people who had crept into a basement or a closet and had lived there undetected for months. Were they missed, she wondered, these trespassers, after they had gone?

She did lose things, and wondered if somehow it was because of all this junk. She kept misplacing the remote control for the television; and she had looked, one night, for her dissertation notes, wondering whether it was too late to try again, but she could not find her notes anywhere; they were not where she thought she had put them. She decided she would have to remind Sylvia about taking the junk away, but then she found the remote control again and forgot all about it.

On a Saturday afternoon in the middle of spring, Sylvia turned up again. After spotting Bonnie through the kitchen window, she came in through the back door without knocking. She was smartly dressed, in the same suit as before, as if it were a uniform, as if she were going to work. The suit matched the colour of her eyes in certain lights, at certain angles. 'Milk and sugar,' she said, handing a shopping bag to Bonnie, who was still in her dressing gown. Bonnie put on the kettle and made two milky, sugary teas, putting Sylvia's in the nicest mug she had, her birthday mug, while Bonnie had the 'I'M A MUG!' mug, which did not look so out of place in her own hands.

Sylvia led the way through to the lounge, where she sat down on the sofa and patted the space beside her. 'Sit down, dear,' she said, and Bonnie sat. Sylvia smiled. 'I've been thinking about your story,' she said. 'The Seatown in your story is fictional. There *is* a place on the Dorset coast called Seatown, but there is no pub there called the Hook, and there is no esplanade as there is in your story. The pub there is called the Anchor, and the shore is a pebble beach enclosed by grey clay cliffs. There is a town called Seaton, just along the coast, in Devon, where there is a pub called the Hook and Parrot, and it does have attic rooms, and there is an esplanade with signs disallowing cycles and dogs and so on. It is not closed on Mondays, though, as your Seatown pub is. There is a pub in Hampshire called the Hook and Glove, which *is* closed on Mondays, and which even has a pig with a chalkboard, although it is not quite like the one in your story. The Hook and Glove, however, is not by the sea.'

'I have been to Seaton,' said Bonnie, 'but the story's just made up.'

'Have you written any more of the story?' asked Sylvia. 'I'd very much like to read it.'

'I haven't,' said Bonnie. 'I haven't written a thing for weeks.'

'Where do you think the anxiety in your writing stems from?' asked Sylvia. 'This obsession with the fragility of limbs?'

'I don't know,' said Bonnie, who had never seen her writing that way. 'I don't *feel* particularly anxious.'

'Well, here and now, you are in a safe and predictable environment. But were you to be *removed* from such a safe and predictable environment, you might expect anxiety levels to rise.'

Bonnie looked anxiously at Sylvia. 'Removed?' she said.

'In your writing, you keep returning to the seaside.'

'I like the seaside,' said Bonnie.

'Some people feel rather trapped by the sea,' suggested Sylvia. 'The seashore is something one cannot go beyond; it hems one in.'

'But you can go beyond it,' said Bonnie. 'You can go to sea; you can go *into* the sea.' It was, for Bonnie, more like the sea was the open side, where structure ceased. The barrier, depending on how you looked at it, both was and was not there, like a theatre's fourth wall, in which case the seaside was the set.

Sylvia clicked her fingers in Bonnie's face. 'Wakey wakey,' she said. She had said something that Bonnie had not caught. When Sylvia had Bonnie's attention again, she continued: 'The excessive anxiety in your writing—'

'Excessive anxiety?'

'Yes,' said Sylvia. '—is perhaps linked to your inability to establish satisfactory conclusions.'

'My inability?'

'Yes,' said Sylvia.

'You know,' said Bonnie, 'for a long time, I had trouble accepting that a storybook's ending was fixed, that it wouldn't change each time I read it, but that it would end how it was always going to end.'

'I think perhaps that follows us even into adulthood,' said Sylvia. 'If I watched *Gone with the Wind* again now, a little part of me would still be hoping that Rhett might stay, that he might change his mind at the very last minute.'

'When I was little,' said Bonnie, 'I had a favourite book, *The Fox and the Hound*, which I asked my mum to read to me over and over again. Then one day, when Mum was away for a few days, my dad read it to me instead, and the story was different. First one dog was killed by a train when it ought to have got away, then the Master gassed a den of kits, then he caught their mother in a trap, then he killed *another* litter of kits after drawing them out of their den, and then he used the sound of a wounded kit to draw out the vixen and killed her; then Copper, the bloodhound, chased Tod until the fox died from exhaustion, and then the Master shot the dog. I told my dad, "That's not how it ends. Tod always escapes, every time. And so do his babies." But Dad said, "No, it goes like this; it ends like this." I told him, "I don't want it to end that way," but Dad just shrugged. "That's what happens," he said, showing me the print on the pages, showing me the black-and-white truth. "You can't change it." Although, of course, Mum *had* changed it, to make it bearable. Even now, when I think of that story, it seems mutable.'

'I used to like *Choose Your Own Adventure* books,' said Sylvia. 'The story could go all sorts of different ways. If you didn't like your ending, you could choose a different one. I even thought of writing one; I thought about becoming a novelist, but I decided that it was all rather pointless. It's hardly saving lives.'

'They changed the story in the film, too,' said Bonnie. 'They made the fox and the hound be friends and no one dies. I prefer the film.'

'You won't remember this,' said Sylvia, like a hypnotist: *When I snap my fingers, you will wake up, and you will remember none of this.* 'You weren't even born, although I suppose you might have seen it anyway. When the *Challenger* failed, when the space shuttle broke apart, my mother videoed it and then rewound the tape to the beginning, ready to show to my father when he came home. All the pieces got pulled back together and the *Challenger* descended safely, intact. It sat on the launch pad, ready and waiting. But as it happened, my father had already seen the footage of the disaster, so neither he nor my mother pressed PLAY.'

'So the shuttle stayed where it was,' said Bonnie, 'on the launch pad.'

'Probably not,' said Sylvia. 'I wouldn't have been able to resist pressing PLAY.'

'I don't think I saw it,' said Bonnie, although even as she said it, she wondered if maybe she had seen the footage after all. She had a flash—somehow simultaneously vague and vivid—of what might have been a memory of some televised disaster, some mid-air disintegration.

Bonnie reached for her pack of cigarettes, which was on top of a magazine on top of a pile of library books on the arm of the sofa. She took from the packet a cigarette and her lighter, put the cigarette between her lips and thumbed the spark wheel of the lighter.

'I'd rather you didn't smoke that in here,' said Sylvia. 'You can smoke in the yard.' She glanced at the magazine on the arm of the sofa; it was turned to the horoscopes at the back. 'You don't read those, do you?' she asked.

'It's often pretty accurate,' said Bonnie. Pulling the magazine onto her lap, she said to Sylvia, 'What star sign are you?'

Sylvia rolled her eyes, leaned closer and read from the page: '"Travel is on the agenda. Embrace your adventurous side. Once you've started there's no going back. You're on the brink of a breakthrough." You know how these things work: it tells you that you'll meet a tall, dark stranger, and then you're on the lookout for a tall, dark stranger. It's a self-fulfilling prophecy—expectation influences behaviour. You know that really, I'm sure.'

'I know,' said Bonnie. 'But even so, it's amazing how often it turns out to be right.'

'It's like anything like that—fortune telling, tarot cards . . . '

'I've got a pack of tarot cards,' said Bonnie. 'But I don't know how to use them.'

'Give them to me,' said Sylvia. Bonnie fetched her tarot cards, broke open the protective cellophane wrapper, and handed the pack over to Sylvia, who shuffled the cards and then cut the deck three times; she seemed to know what she was doing. Holding the pack out to Bonnie, she said, 'Take a card from the top and place it face up between us.' Bonnie did so, and they both looked at it and saw that it was the Tower, tall and grey with small, high windows, and behind it was the pitch-black night sky, and beneath it were jagged rocks towards which were falling two surprised-looking figures. 'So,' said Sylvia. 'You go to a tarot reader and you turn over the Tower. You are told that this card means danger; sudden and destructive change. You turned it over, you attracted that card, so now you are certain that that's what's coming your way: danger, sudden and destructive change. And because you are literal minded, you are thinking about yourself falling from a great height, a high window, something like that. The card, the Tower, has as good as told you that this is what is going to happen. You know it is going to happen. It is there in your future—you've seen it illustrated in full colour.' Sylvia tapped the Tower card with her index finger. 'And even if the tarot reader tells you that this future is not set in stone, and that you can avoid such an eventuality, still you will find yourself circling it, this idea of the Tower, a building with high windows, from which you will fall.' Bonnie had barely blinked while Sylvia had been speaking; she was gazing intently at Sylvia, whose eyes were the colour of deep water. 'You will be drawn towards this destiny like water to a plughole, swirling down.' Sylvia sat back and smiled. 'That's how diets work as well, of course,' she said. 'A magazine tells you—and you say to yourself— *Do not eat the cake*. That cake now has a label attached to it, which says, 'DON'T EAT ME'. This label, I think, is far more powerful than the label on Alice in Wonderland's cake, which says, 'EAT ME', and on her drink which says, 'DRINK ME'. 'DON'T EAT ME' says this cake, which you can't see because you've put it somewhere safe but you know it is there and it is still making your mouth water. 'DON'T EAT ME,' says the cake, and you will indeed not eat the cake for as long as you possibly can, all the time with one eye—your mind's eye—on where you have put your cake, or trying *so hard not* to look at it, not even to think about it, right up until the moment when, of course, you will not only look at it but *you will finally give in and eat it*.'

Sylvia looked at her watch. 'I have to go,' she said. 'Besides, it's a Saturday evening. You'll be off out somewhere, I expect.'

'I'll see you out,' said Bonnie, and she made her way through to the kitchen. 'There are other Bonnies,' she said, 'as well as Bonnie Parker and *My Bonnie lies over the ocean*.

There's Bonnie Tyler, and Bonnie Langford, and Bonnie Greer.' She was at the back door before she realised that Sylvia was not behind her, and it was if Bonnie were the one leaving somebody else's house. Sylvia came into the kitchen a moment later, carrying the dirty mugs that Bonnie had left behind on the carpet. 'There are other Bonnies,' said Bonnie.

'Of course,' said Sylvia. 'There aren't very many of you though, are there? The name's not popular these days. It's gone out of fashion. You're an endangered species.' She put the mugs down on the side, finding a space near the sink. 'You could do with some proper teacups,' she said. 'Thin china cups. It makes the tea taste better.'

At the door, Sylvia paused and said to Bonnie, 'You're afraid of your own story. But you don't need to worry about what happens at the end. All you need to know is: *What happens next?*'

After Sylvia had gone, Bonnie smoked her cigarette in the doorway and then locked up. She got herself some supper to take to bed: some warm milk, which would help her to sleep, and some cheese, which would give her weird dreams. On her way through to the bedroom, she stopped off in the lounge to take her Seatown story out of the drawer. She wondered about her anxiety, her obsession with the fragility of limbs. She did remember being frightened of a busker whose legs could bend the wrong way, and having a nightmare after seeing a dog that had wheels instead of back legs. She thought about her story and how it might end. She thought, *What happens next?* She remembered something that Sylvia had said to her: 'In your writing, you keep returning to the seaside.' Had Sylvia seen her other unfinished stories? Bonnie looked in the drawer but all her printouts were there, including, in fact, her dissertation notes.

Bonnie went through to her bedroom, which was dark, and into which a blade of light was coming beneath the locked door. She thought of the bunch of keys attached to the belt loop of Sylvia's skirt. She thought about moving the furniture, pushing the wardrobe or the bed in front of the door. But whatever she did was likely to make no difference at all, she realised, because Sylvia probably still had her own key to the back door.

II

7

L EAVING BEHIND THE blank—though perhaps not entirely blank—piece of paper, Susan went downstairs, to the landlady's rooms on the next landing. After knocking on the solid wooden door, she waited. After a minute, the landlady came to the door wearing an apron that said, 'I'M THE BOSS!' She was a strikingly tall woman, and under her apron she was smartly dressed, in an outfit that matched her eyeshadow and complemented the colour of her eyes, which were the shifting blue-grey-green of the sea and reminded Susan of childhood beach holidays and almost drowning.

'Did you come up to my room just now?' asked Susan. 'I'm afraid I didn't hear anyone knocking. I was sleeping.'

'No,' said the landlady. 'I've not been up to your room today. I've been baking.'

'Someone's been up to my room,' said Susan.

'I don't think so,' said the landlady. 'You know the pub's closed. It's only you and me here today.'

'Somebody put something under my door,' said Susan.

'Put what under your door?' asked the landlady.

'A piece of paper,' said Susan. 'I assumed it was a note for me.'

'What does it say?'

'I'm not sure,' said Susan. 'I'm not sure it says anything.'

The landlady gave her a strange look. 'Where is this note?' she asked.

'I left it in my room,' said Susan.

'I'll come and have a look,' said the landlady.

A beeping sound came from the kitchen and the landlady held up a finger to Susan: *Wait.* She went back into her kitchen and opened the oven door. Susan caught the edge of a baking smell that made her mouth water. A moment later, the beeping sound was turned off and the landlady came out again still wearing her 'I'M THE BOSS!' apron. 'Right,' she said, touching Susan's elbow to steer her towards the stairs. 'Show me this piece of paper.'

She followed Susan up the stairs and into her room, where Susan looked for the piece of paper on the desk by the door. There was some writing paper on the desk, but not that same scrap. She looked on the floor, and on the bedside table, and on and in the bed. 'It was here,' she said. 'But now I can't see it.'

'I'm sure it will turn up,' said the landlady.

The beeping sound came again, up the stairs or through the floorboards, and Susan's mouth watered. 'That will be my scones,' said the landlady. 'Come with me.' Susan locked the door to her room and followed the landlady back down the stairs. 'Wait there,' said the landlady. Susan waited on the landing. From there, and indeed from outside her own room, she could see over the banister to the ground floor, the hardwood staircase spiralling down, framing the cramped entrance hall, the floor tiles off-white with occasional squares of red. When Susan looked at it from the top floor, she thought of the life nets or jumping sheets that firefighters used, or once used, and she felt the pull of the drop.

The landlady came back with a few hot scones around which she was wrapping a clean tea towel. 'Go and get some fresh air,' she said.

Susan headed down the stairs and went outside. Her bundle of scones wrapped in a checked tea towel made her feel like a runaway setting out for London, like Oliver Twist running away from the undertaker's with a crust of bread and a coarse shirt and a penny tied up in a handkerchief. She sat down on a bench in front of the pub. There were very few people around—she could see a couple at the seashore with a toddler on reins, and a bald man coming along the esplanade. The bald man seemed to say something to the family, and the couple turned around and looked at him but did not reply. It was late in the day, as well as late in the year, and there was not much light left. Susan opened up the tea towel and began to eat one of the scones, which was surprisingly dense. She was not looking at the bald man when he stopped just in front of her and leaned against the railings in between Susan and the sea. With her mouth full of scone, she became aware of him standing there, staring at her. His arms, holding on to the railings behind him, were bent at an odd, double-jointed angle. 'Jump!' he said, and Susan looked right at him. She saw the smooth, flat space between his unblinking eyes and his unsmiling mouth, and saw that he was not looking at her after all; those eyes were only tattoos on the back of his head, and the thin, wide mouth was a crease in the skin at the base of his skull. He was facing the sea; and as commanded, a dog that had been hidden from Susan's view by the sea wall jumped up from the beach onto the esplanade, and the man let go of the railings and turned away from the beach. He did not look at her, but the dog did; the dog saw her. The man strolled on down the esplanade, with the dog trotting along at his heels. From her place on the bench, Susan watched him go, and the tattooed eyes in the back of his head stared unblinkingly back at her.

In the middle of the night, Susan woke suddenly from a dream in which she was driving. An instructor was in the passenger seat. He had dual controls, pedals that Susan could not see, but the pressing of which she could feel influencing her control of the car. The driving instructor's eyes were those same tattooed eyes, and the place where his nose belonged was smooth and flat, and his mouth was thin-lipped and wide and unsmiling. He was turned towards her, looking steadily at her, but he did not speak to her at all. Somehow, though, he was instructing her nonetheless, and had told her which way to go. Susan had circled a roundabout, and as she left it, she realised that this exit was going to send her hurtling south when she had expected to go north. Either the driving instructor had misdirected her or Susan had acted contrary to his instructions. It was going to be difficult for her to get back onto the northbound side of the motorway.

She lay, open-eyed now, facing the black rectangle of the uncurtained window in the far wall. The window was closed, so that the roaring and crashing of the sea would not disturb her while she was sleeping.

She could see, in the middle of the dark windowpane, a smaller, white square. She sat up, peering at it, trying to see what it was: not the moon, a square moon; if she moved her head she could see the moon, a white circle beside the white square, like a geometry test. There was a framed, glazed picture on the opposite wall, but it did not seem to be a reflection of that. Pushing back the duvet, she climbed out of bed and crossed the room without switching on the light. At the window, she reached out and touched the white square. It was a sheet of paper, stuck to the inside of the glass. On it, she thought she saw, despite the darkness, a word: 'JUMP'. She unstuck the paper from the window, took it over to the desk and switched on the lamp, but when she looked at the paper in the light, she found that there was nothing written on it after all, or else the message had simply vanished, as happened, for example, when she wrote with her finger in condensation on a window, and then the condensation evaporated, leaving behind only a trace of what had been there, the unseen shape of her writing on the glass, and then sometimes it reappeared.

She switched the lamp off again and looked at the page in darkness as before—as if it might be some kind of glow-in-the-dark trick—but still she could see nothing there. She wondered if it was the same piece of paper as the one that had been slipped under her door and then lost; but whether it was the same piece of paper or not, who would or could have stuck it to her window?

Keeping the light off, so that she would not feel exposed to the outside world, she went to her door and opened it, looking out and towards the stairs, but there was no one there. 'Hello?' she called, but very quietly. She closed the door again. She went to the wardrobe and flung open the double doors, so that the empty hangers rattled. She got down on her knees and peered under her bed, looking right into the corners. She felt like her own mother trying to prove to her that there were no monsters hiding anywhere in her bedroom. It was really too dark to see clearly though, and she did not turn her lamp on again, and she did not stretch out an arm to feel around in the darkness under the bed.

She screwed up the piece of paper and threw it into the wastepaper basket. She half-expected that in the morning she would not find it in there, that this was only some kind of bad dream or depths-of-the-night confusion. She went back to bed. She thought she might lie awake until it got light, but she must have fallen straight back to sleep because later she woke and it was still dark and there, again, in the middle of the black rectangle of the window, was a small, white square. She wondered if this was one of those dreams that she sometimes got stuck in, which she might 'wake' from, and then find that she had only made it into the next part of the dream. Then, when she really did wake up, she could not quite trust it; she could not quite believe in the realness of her life.

She stared at the white square. She closed her eyes for a moment, but when she opened them again she was still in the same dream, or else wide awake. She got up and crossed the room, reaching out for the piece of paper that was stuck to the glass, to unstick it, and found that she could not: her fingers slipped right over it as if it were frozen in ice. The piece of paper was now stuck to the *outside* of the glass. It was like a blank picture, mounted on the black of endless sky and endless sea; it was like Tom Friedman's *1000 Hours of Staring*, bare paper impregnated with the artist's purposeful staring, the artwork's medium listed as 'stare on paper'; or it was like Gianni Motti's *Magic Ink* series of drawings which were done, according to the artist, in invisible ink that had disappeared on completion of the work.

Susan opened the window and peered out, as if she might find some joker halfway down a ladder, or see someone running off down the street, but there was no ladder and nobody running away.

It would not be possible, she thought, for her to reach around to the middle of the outside of the window, so instead she inspected the piece of paper from her side of the glass. There did seem to be something written on it, but it was not quite legible; it was as if the message had been left out in the rain and had all but washed away. But she thought that perhaps she could almost make out one word, or a half-perceived whisper of the word: 'JUMP'.

Through the open window, she could hear the sea washing in and out, rattling the stones at the shore and dragging the smaller ones out. She could see the dark line that the deep sea made against the night sky, like a streak of black ink on black paper.

She closed the window again. If she'd had curtains she would have drawn them. She went back to bed and lay awake listening, without knowing quite what she was listening for—a creak that might just be this old building settling, some rustling or scratching in a corner that might be mice, a breath that might just be a gust coming in through a gap in the window frame.

8

THE WEATHER HAD turned warmer, and Bonnie had taken to sitting out in the backyard, a concreted sun-trap, through whose cracks the weeds grew and to whose low end wall the landlady had attached a trellis for clematis and wisteria to climb up.

Bonnie read horror and fantasy novels from the library, and women's magazines, or she just sat and watched the birds fly overhead, or she watched the clouds change shape as they drifted across the blue sky.

On this particular Saturday, she was sitting out there with Sylvia, both of them in deckchairs. They had slipped off their shoes—Bonnie could see Sylvia's neatly painted toenails—and they had bared their legs below the knee. Bonnie felt like they ought to be eating ice creams, or fish and chips.

'I feel like we ought to be able to hear seagulls,' said Bonnie.

'It's possible to buy recordings of seagulls' cries,' said Sylvia.

'Is it?' said Bonnie.

Having become aware that Bonnie had written a further two thousand words of her Seatown story, Sylvia had been nagging Bonnie to let her read this next installment, and it had not taken very long for Bonnie to give in. Now Bonnie was waiting for Sylvia to finish reading the new pages, and it felt a bit like lying down while a doctor inspected her soft insides and she waited for it to hurt. In fact, Bonnie had a vague idea that Sylvia had mentioned doing a PhD, in which case perhaps she *was* a doctor, but either way, she was not a *real* doctor.

Bonnie could see exactly which line Sylvia was reading—*she could hear the sea washing in and out, rattling the stones at the shore and dragging the smaller ones out*—because she moved her left thumb down the side of the page as she went, as if she were checking it, looking for errors. Sylvia came to the end of the page and said, 'Yes, you can get CDs with all sorts of sound effects on.'

Bonnie reached out for her story but Sylvia kept hold of it.

'Have you ever held a conch shell to your ear to hear the sound of the sea?' asked Sylvia.

'I have tried it,' said Bonnie, 'but I could never find one that worked.'

'You know it's not the shell,' said Sylvia, looking at her, 'don't you?'

'Yes,' said Bonnie. She did know that really; she knew that it was all to do with the shutting out of external sounds, and resonance, and that what you heard, that sound of the sea, was partly just the sound of your own blood flowing. But still, she remembered being on beaches, picking up shells and trying them out, wanting to hear the rushing in and crashing and drawing out of the sea, and she never could; she never could hear what everyone else seemed to hear in those shells.

'Your teacup,' said Sylvia, nodding at the empty cup at Bonnie's feet, 'would work just as well, or your hand cupped over your ear.' Bonnie cupped both hands over her ears and tried

70

to hear the sea. She thought that perhaps she could *almost* hear it; there was a distant rumble. She took her hands away from her ears and Sylvia said, 'Where was it that you almost drowned?'

'I jumped off the end of a pier in Blackpool,' said Bonnie.

'How old were you?' asked Sylvia.

'Nine or ten,' said Bonnie, 'something like that.'

'That would have been after I last saw you and your mother,' said Sylvia. 'What made you do it?'

Bonnie frowned and scratched her arm with bitten fingernails. 'I'm not sure. I don't really remember doing it. I remember being on the pier, and I remember the railings, and I remember landing in the water, going under.'

'And you almost drowned?'

'Well, no, not really,' said Bonnie. 'I could swim. I swallowed a lot of seawater though, swimming to the shore. My dad was standing there waiting for me. "One of these days . . . " he said. I don't remember what, or even if he told me. "One of these days," though, he said.'

'Where was your mother?' asked Sylvia.

'She was still up on the pier,' said Bonnie, 'looking down at where I'd jumped in. She was probably wondering whether she should go in after me.'

'But she didn't?'

'No,' said Bonnie. 'She took me for my first cup of tea. We didn't go back onto the pier after that.' She picked up the pack of cigarettes that was in her lap, and lit one. 'But Blackpool has three piers,' she added. 'The second time might have been there as well.'

'The second time?' said Sylvia. 'You've done it more than once?'

'Yes,' said Bonnie. 'And after Blackpool, there was Bognor Regis.' On Bognor's stunted pier, she had seen the sea—green

71

like cats' eyes—between the planks beneath her feet, and the railings had been like a silver ladder. 'And then Belgium Pier in Blankenberge.' She remembered a semi-circular wooden ledge around the end of the pier in Blankenberge, with words carved into it, Flemish perhaps, which she could not understand. The ledge was wide enough to sit on. She could feel—against her bare skin while she sat with her legs dangling over the water—the shape of the words in the timber.

'What if the tide had been out?' said Sylvia. 'Would you still have jumped? And what if you had landed on rocks?'

Bonnie shrugged. 'After a while, we stopped going to resorts that had piers. That's probably when we first went to Seaton, which doesn't have a pier.'

Sylvia leafed through the pages of the story. 'I don't like the bit about the man with tattooed eyes,' she said. 'I'm not sure it's necessary. Is this someone you've actually seen?'

Bonnie reached across again and took her story out of Sylvia's hands. 'There was a teacher at school,' she said, 'who had this really thick, dark hair. Then he got his head shaved for charity, and when all the hair came off, you could see the pair of eyes that had been underneath, tattooed onto his scalp. They were really creepy, but he kept his head shaved after that because when he was teaching, none of the kids ever messed around behind his back, because the eyes were always watching them.'

'But they knew, of course, that these eyes were only tattoos?'

'Yes,' said Bonnie, 'but it worked anyway. It's like how cardboard policemen in shops deter shoplifters.'

'Have you ever actually thought,' said Sylvia, with a smile, 'that there were monsters under your bed?'

'I did used to have to get my mum to look under there,' said Bonnie, 'otherwise I couldn't get to sleep.'

'Did you know,' said Sylvia, 'that there are stories of psychologists or researchers gathering data by hiding under people's beds, without their subjects' knowledge?'

'Surely not,' said Bonnie. 'That doesn't sound like something that would be allowed.'

'This was in the 1930s,' said Sylvia. 'It wouldn't be allowed now.'

Bonnie dropped the end of her cigarette onto the ground. Out of habit, she would have ground it out with her heel, and her bare foot did twitch towards it, but she left it smouldering. She glanced at her watch. It was three o'clock. 'It's really too hot for tea,' she said, leaning down and picking up the empty cups at their feet. 'But I'm going to put the kettle on anyway.'

From the kitchen, Bonnie could hear the television that she had left on in the lounge. She often left it on the twenty-four-hour news channel, so that there was a permanent background murmur of reporting, the same stories repeating throughout the day, the same headlines flashing up on the screen. Occasionally, in amongst the tragedies, there were reports of survivors: a newborn baby found alive after five days alone down a storm drain; people rescued from rubble after nearly a week, nearly two weeks, nearly three weeks; a cat rescued from a storage container after a month of living on nothing but condensation; a man found clinging to the hull of his upturned boat after sixty-six days adrift at sea; another man who drifted across the Pacific Ocean for four hundred and thirty-eight days before being washed ashore, thousands of miles from home. Bonnie could have put all these stories into a scrapbook; she could have had a book in which everyone survived.

The kettle worked itself up to a boil and Bonnie made the tea.

Returning to Sylvia with the two full cups, Bonnie said, 'I'm going out for a meal next week, for my thirtieth birthday. It's not actually my birthday any more but nobody could make it on the day, so we're going out next Saturday. Would you like to come?'

'I would rather like that,' said Sylvia. 'I'd like to meet your friends.'

Bonnie passed her one of the teas. 'Cheers,' she said, and Sylvia said, 'Good health,' and they touched the rims of their cups together, although the tea was too hot yet so they did not drink the toast.

When the sun began to sink, Sylvia went back to her own flat, and Bonnie remained in the backyard watching the warm light go out of the evening, watching the sky whiten and then faintly purple, like a wash of watercolour, like Dulux Violet White. The trees turned black and looked, thought Bonnie, like something designed by Tim Burton. Her skin cooled. She felt comfortable, and it was an effort to get out of the deckchair and into her bed, and then when she was in bed she could not sleep. She put her coat on over her nightie and walked to the all-night garage, where she bought a bar of chocolate, and opened it on the way home. She did not see a soul apart from the cashier who dealt with her through the night hatch; and a strange man, tall and dark in the darkness, waiting outside her house, holding a briefcase. She almost said to him, 'Are you looking for me?' But before she had swallowed her chocolate, the sound of an approaching bus made her turn around. The last bus of the night drew to a squealing halt at the stop outside the house. The man got on and the bus took him away.

9

A T THE LAB, Chi was increasingly absent. She had begun to miss days and then whole weeks. 'Where's Chichi?' Mr Carr would say. 'Why isn't Chichi here?' Bonnie did not know why, and Mr Carr would say, 'Fat lot of use you are.' Bonnie was given Chi's work to do, alongside her own, although she would not be paid for doing both. She cleaned Chi's offices, and the canteen, on whose herringbone parquet floor she had to use the buffer, a machine that Bonnie found frightening: it seemed to have the potential waywardness of a shopping trolley, as well as a surprisingly powerful motor.

When Chi reappeared after a few days or a week or more, she said that she had been ill, but she received warnings, given by Mr Carr behind closed doors. Bonnie had also had warnings, both for being late and sometimes for not turning up. 'I thought you were the reliable one, Chichi,' said Mr Carr, shaking his head in disappointment at seeing Chi arrive late again. 'But now,' he said, cocking his thumb towards Bonnie, 'you're worse than her.'

One Monday, Chi was gone and someone else was there in her place. The new worker introduced herself to Bonnie as Fiona, although Mr Carr called her Chichi, as if this were a soap opera in which an actor had left but the character continued and the rest of the cast had to carry on as if nothing had changed.

Fiona was small and slim, with dark hair so thick that it might have been a wig. Dressed all in black, wearing leggings and trainers, she looked like she was ready to run, or like she could sink into the shadows and just disappear.

On Fiona's first day, while she and Bonnie were in the staff room and Bonnie was reading the terms and conditions on the back of a packet of sweets, Fiona suddenly said, 'Dare,' making Bonnie look up. 'I dare you,' said Fiona, and she glanced around the room. Her gaze settled on Mr Carr's coat, a padded jacket hanging on a nearby hook. 'I dare you,' she said, 'to spit in Mr Carr's coat pocket.'

'What?' said Bonnie.

'You heard me,' said Fiona.

Bonnie looked at Mr Carr's coat; she looked at the pocket. This was a game that had always made Bonnie nervous. At school, it had been Truth, Dare, Double Dare, Love, Kiss or Promise, although, even then, it had seemed mostly to be Dare, or Double Dare which was worse. Once, for a Double Dare, Bonnie had climbed up onto the roof of the sports hut, from which she had been dared to jump. Bonnie had gone to the nearest edge and stood there, looking down, and then someone had shouted up to her and she had jumped. Landing awkwardly on a hard patch of ground, she had twisted her ankle. The teacher on duty in the playground had taken one look at Bonnie and told her that she was a stupid girl. Bonnie had been taken to see the school nurse, who sat Bonnie down, asked her where she had hurt herself and what had happened, tended to the injury and called her a very stupid girl. 'Erica dared me to do it,' said Bonnie. The nurse peered over her half-moon spectacles. 'And if Erica dared you to jump off a skyscraper,' said the nurse, 'would you do it?' Bonnie pictured herself standing on the roof of a skyscraper, her toes right up against a concrete edge, or hanging over it, like someone about to dive into a swimming pool, her head tipped forward to see the ground far below, gravity compelling her. *Dare.* In the nurse's room, Bonnie felt a twinge in her ankle and closed her eyes. At home time, her mother was waiting for her at the school gates. As she helped Bonnie into the car, she said, 'You are a stupid girl.'

Bonnie stood up and went over to where Mr Carr's coat was hanging up, and touched the pocket.

'What do you think you're doing?' said Mr Carr, coming into the room.

'Nothing,' said Bonnie, taking her fingers away from his pocket, stepping away from his coat.

Mr Carr looked at her, came over and looked in the pocket of his coat. He narrowed his eyes at her, came very close and said quietly, 'Whatever you're thinking, don't.' He looked at his watch. 'What are you standing around in here for?' he said. 'You're slack, do you know that? You ought to have started work five minutes ago.'

Bonnie stood rooted to the spot, waiting for him to finish.

Mr Carr clicked his fingers in her face. 'Chop chop,' he said. 'When I say jump, you jump.'

Bonnie went off to her corridors, and Fiona made her way to the offices.

Dare was Fiona's favourite game. At any moment, Fiona might say, 'Dare.' She might say it as soon as Bonnie came in through the gates, or she might say it during a pause in conversation in the staff room, or sometimes entire weeks would go by and then she would say it: 'Dare,' as if they were constantly in the game; as if they were only ever resting in between bouts. With no preamble at all, she would say, 'Dare,' and it was, thought Bonnie, like a posthypnotic cue; her new friend would say, 'Dare,' and Bonnie would do what she said, or at least she would attempt to.

'Dare,' said Fiona, and Bonnie might have to get something out of the vending machine without paying for it, or she would have to get the security guard on the gate to agree to a date. Bonnie hated doing these dares, and yet, when dared, she could not resist, although ultimately she always failed; she never seemed to have the knack for getting free stuff out of the machine or whatever it was.

'I dare you,' said Fiona, one breezy Friday evening, 'to get into one of the labs and let an animal out of its cage.' Bonnie hated to think about those cages, which she had never seen but which she knew must exist inside the laboratories behind the double doors. She was tempted.

She began her shift, fetching and filling a bucket and carrying it carefully to her starting point. She moved slowly down the long corridor, mopping away the day's footprints. When she came to the first set of double doors, she paused. She did not know who might be in there. She never saw anyone around that late in the day, apart from her own cleaning team, and the security guard on the gate, reading his paper.

Taking one hand off the mop, she reached out and touched the door. She did not know what she might find behind it. She thought about films she had seen, like *28 Days Later* in which the release of infected chimps caused the spread of a highly contagious virus. She was afraid of what she might unleash.

She pushed against the door but it did not open; she pushed a little bit harder but it appeared to be locked. She continued down the corridor, mopping from side to side with the warm, bleach-scented water, pausing occasionally to refresh and wring the mop, glancing again at the shut-tight doors behind her.

Back in the staff room at the end of the shift, Fiona was sitting drinking a can of Coca-Cola from the vending machine. She raised her eyebrows at Bonnie, and the eyebrows said, *Did you do it?*

'The lab was locked,' said Bonnie.

'Fail,' said Fiona, lifting a right-angled thumb and forefinger to her forehead. The thumb and forefinger said, *Loser*, and Fiona said, 'Loser.' She passed the can to Bonnie, who took a few sips, and the drink made her teeth feel soft.

Mr Carr came into the room. 'All right, girls?' he said and Fiona rolled her eyes. Mr Carr stopped at the vending machine to get an energy drink. With the can in his hand, he turned to face Fiona and Bonnie before opening it. He stood with his legs wide apart and drank it down in one go, crushing the empty can in his fist when he had finished and throwing it overarm into a bin on the far side of the room.

Fiona got to her feet and shrugged on her coat, and Mr Carr said, 'Come on then, girls,' and he came over and furtled around in their bags and pockets, and then he let them go.

They walked towards the gate, and Fiona said, 'Mr Carr's a jerk. He tried to feel me up in the store room.'

'You're kidding,' said Bonnie.

'Has he ever done that to you?' asked Fiona.

'No,' said Bonnie, reaching into her bag for her cigarettes. 'You ought to report him.'

'Don't worry,' said Fiona. 'I'll take care of him.'

Bonnie put a cigarette in her mouth, and Fiona gave her a look of disappointment, which Bonnie was used to.

'Don't you know they'll kill you?' said Fiona.

'I know,' said Bonnie, 'but I can't seem to quit.'

'Have you really tried, though?' asked Fiona, but Bonnie was turning away, out of the wind, trying to light her cigarette with an unresponsive lighter. Finally, a flame appeared and Bonnie lit her cigarette.

'You really shouldn't smoke,' said Fiona.

'I know,' said Bonnie, sucking down the tarry smoke. 'I know.'

Out on the street, Bonnie said to Fiona, 'I don't know where you live.'

'I live with my boyfriend,' said Fiona, gesturing so vaguely that even the direction was not clear.

'I don't live far away,' said Bonnie, 'if you want to come round some time, any time.'

'OK,' said Fiona, 'thanks,' but she did not ask Bonnie for her address or her phone number. 'Well, maybe see you on Monday,' she said.

'But I'll see you on Saturday, won't I?' said Bonnie. 'For my birthday get-together?'

'Is that this weekend?' said Fiona. 'I forgot. Where is it again? What time?'

Bonnie told her. 'You don't have to bring a present,' she added, but Fiona was already putting in her earphones, raising a hand as she turned and walked away.

Bonnie put in her own earphones and turned on her iPod. She selected her French language course and walked home, listening to the declining of verbs—*je peux, tu peux, il peut*—in a language with which she could not get to grips.

BONNIE WAS RUNNING late. She and Sylvia were supposed to have left for the restaurant already, for Bonnie's birthday celebration, but while Sylvia was ready and waiting in the lounge, Bonnie was only just out of the shower, not yet dressed, her hair still damp and tangled.

In her bedroom, Bonnie rummaged through her wardrobe. Nothing seemed quite right. She took a recent charity-shop acquisition off its hanger and held it up against herself in front of the mirror, wondering why on earth she had bought it. She put it back in her wardrobe. There was a nasty spot on her chin but she was resisting the urge to squeeze it because that would only make things worse, make the blemish more visible; she would use some concealer instead, and she would use the eyeshadow that her mother said was needed to draw attention away from her jaw, and her nose.

Finally, she made it into the lounge, holding a piece of tissue to her chin where she had given in and squeezed the pustule, and Sylvia looked at her and said, 'You really don't need make-up. Or not so much.'

By the time they left the flat, they ought already to have been at the restaurant, and even then Bonnie had to go back inside to look for her door key, and in the end Sylvia said,

'Never mind, I've got one, let's just go.'

As they hurried through the passageway, Sylvia, looking at the neckline of Bonnie's strappy dress, said, 'You're going to be cold,' but there was no time to turn back.

'Where exactly is this restaurant?' asked Sylvia.

'I think I know,' said Bonnie. It was a Chinese restaurant, to which she had been once before, some years ago, perhaps for her eighteenth birthday, or her twenty-first: a landmark birthday, which at the time had felt like passing through a portal, as if everything would be different on the other side. New Year's Eves were like that: at the end of the countdown, she always felt as if she ought to hold her breath, ready to jump, braced for the cold or a hard landing.

The restaurant had gone. Bonnie walked past where it ought to have been, twice, but it seemed to have metamorphosed into a chip shop. They were terribly late now. She walked to the end of the road, where cars were whipping past on the dual carriageway. She turned back. 'It's just not here!' she protested, as if this were some kind of trick.

She found the restaurant eventually, in the middle of an adjacent street. The bright facade, red for luck, was the same as the original, as if it had just been lifted off, moved to a unit in the next street along, and stuck back on again, like a structure in a Potemkin village.

Inside the restaurant, the layout and decor looked much the same as it always had, in the other location, as if in fact the building had just been wheeled wholesale down the street.

They were led by a white-jacketed waiter to a booth at the back of the restaurant, where they found their party eating, nearing the end of a course. Bonnie's father looked up and said, 'You're late.' He put his last piece of chicken in his mouth and pushed away his empty plate.

'Sorry,' said Bonnie. 'I couldn't find the restaurant. It's moved.'

'Oh,' said her mother, 'yes, it has,' as if that was not very important, as if buildings moved about all the time and you just had to keep up.

'This is my friend Sylvia,' said Bonnie, presenting her landlady with a flourish, as if she were the grand reveal at the end of a magic show. Bonnie's mother was busy passing some sauce across the table, but turned and offered her hand to Sylvia when Bonnie said, 'This is my mum . . . and my dad . . . and this is Fiona, my friend from work.' Fiona said hello but she looked annoyed, as if she wished she were elsewhere. 'Sorry we're late,' said Bonnie.

Bonnie sat down next to Fiona, and Sylvia sat next to Bonnie, boxing her into the booth.

'We've had our starters,' said Bonnie's father. 'And we ordered our mains as well.'

'I'm sure it's not too late to add yours on though,' said Bonnie's mother, 'but they might come out a bit later.'

'All right,' said Bonnie, and she glanced through the menu and then looked around, trying to catch a waiter's eye.

'Mrs Falls,' said Sylvia, smoothing out a crease in the tablecloth, 'Bonnie tells me that you ski.'

'That's right,' said Bonnie's mother. 'I like to compete.'

'I ski as well,' said Bonnie's father.

'And when you go skiing,' said Sylvia to Bonnie's mother, 'you don't have a problem with the heights? You've never . . . had an accident?'

'We did have a twisted ankle,' said Bonnie's mother.

'Oh yes?'

'But that wasn't on the slopes. It was on a slippery poolside that you twisted your ankle, wasn't it?' she said to Bonnie's father.

'I'd just done my mile of swimming,' he said.

'All right,' said Sylvia. 'And when you compete,' she said to Bonnie's mother, 'you have some success?'

'Oh yes,' said Bonnie's father. 'We had to buy a whole new cabinet for all Pearl's trophies. It's in pride of place in the spare room. That's your old room, Bonnie.'

Bonnie had not yet managed to attract the attention of a waiter, and in the end, her mother turned her head as a waiter came by and she stopped him. 'My daughter is ready to order now,' she said, and as Bonnie and Sylvia ordered their food, the rest of the meals came out and the three of them tucked in.

Bonnie's father, eyeing Fiona's progress, said, 'You eat a lot for a little girl.'

'I'm not a little girl,' said Fiona.

'You are,' he said. He turned to Bonnie's mother and said, 'Isn't she? Whereas our Bonnie's always been a big girl.'

'She's hardly a girl,' said Fiona. 'She's thirty years old.'

'That's right,' he said, turning to Bonnie. 'Tick tock.'

He picked up the bottle of table wine and filled Bonnie's mother's glass, and then Sylvia's, and then Fiona's. Bonnie poured herself a glass of water.

'Aren't you having wine?' asked Sylvia.

'I don't drink,' said Bonnie.

'Not even on your birthday?' said Sylvia.

'I prefer not to,' said Bonnie.

'My mother doesn't drink,' said Fiona. 'She's one of these high-powered people who doesn't like to lose control.' They all looked at Bonnie, whose hair, though dry, was still tangled, and whose dress looked like cats had been sitting on it, even though she did not have a cat.

'Not even one little glass?' asked Sylvia. 'Just a sip?'

Bonnie shook her head and reached for her water.

'Well,' said Sylvia, 'many happy returns anyway,' and the four of them touched their wine glasses desultorily against Bonnie's water glass.

Sylvia's dinner arrived, though not Bonnie's, and when the waiter came back to take away the empty plates, Bonnie's mother asked him where Bonnie's dinner had got to. The waiter went to check and after a while he returned to say that there had been some mistake and that no other order had gone through to the kitchen. The order was placed again. 'And the bill, please,' said Bonnie's father.

When the waiter had dealt with the bill and had gone away again, Sylvia said to Bonnie's parents, 'I've been reading some of Bonnie's writing.'

'It's about time she gave that up,' said her father. 'I've told her, writing is a young man's game. A writer will always do his best work before he's thirty, and after that it's just so much hogwash.'

'One of Bonnie's stories,' said Sylvia, 'touches on a phase she went through of jumping off the ends of piers, in Blackpool and Bognor Regis and Belgium.'

Bonnie's father looked at Bonnie and shook his head in astonishment, as if, once again, she stood dripping and bedraggled before him. 'She took a long walk on a short pier,' he said. He tapped his temple with his index finger and said to Sylvia, 'She hasn't got a bit of sense.'

'It's just as well the tide was in,' said Bonnie's mother, 'otherwise she'd have broken her legs, if she was lucky.'

'And she used to sleepwalk,' mentioned Sylvia, 'and nearly

went out of a window?'

'She's like a bloody lemming,' said Bonnie's father.

'Don't you ever feel,' said Bonnie, 'when you're up high—'

'Don't mumble,' said Sylvia.

'She does mumble, doesn't she?' said Bonnie's mother.

'When you're up high,' said Bonnie, 'don't you ever feel an urge to jump? Don't you ever feel that you might not be able to stop yourself?'

Sylvia smiled, and Bonnie's father touched his fingertip to his temple again.

'Freud wrote about the death drive,' said Sylvia, 'a death instinct, leading organic life back into the inanimate state.'

'What do you do for a living, Sylvia?' asked Bonnie's mother.

'I'm just a landlady,' said Sylvia, 'now.'

Bonnie's mother ate a mint and said, 'Well, we could go if it wasn't for Bonnie's dinner.'

They talked a little longer, and finally Bonnie's dinner arrived. 'Eat up,' said her father, and her mother started putting on her coat. Bonnie ate her chips and drank her water while everyone waited, and then her father said, 'All right, let's go.'

Bonnie's mother handed Bonnie a mint and said, 'Have one of these. It will help with your breath.'

Outside the restaurant, Bonnie's parents said their good-byes and drove home, and Sylvia said to Fiona, 'Whereabouts do you live?' but Fiona was evasive. She went one way— 'Maybe see you on Monday,' she said—while Bonnie and Sylvia went the other.

It had grown unexpectedly dark while they had been inside. Bonnie was feeling the cold; as they passed the end of Waterside Close, she shivered, and Sylvia, who had been walking along quietly, seeming deep in thought, said, 'Do you have any plans for the summer? Are you going away anywhere?'

'I'd like to go somewhere,' said Bonnie. 'A few years ago, I stayed in an Ibis hotel and that was really nice. Apparently they have them abroad too. I'd like to try one of those sometime.'

'They're all the same, you know,' said Sylvia. 'You could be anywhere.'

'They're not *exactly* the same,' said Bonnie.

'There's a hotel in Japan,' said Sylvia, 'whose reception desk is staffed by a team of identical robots that look completely real.'

'Really?' said Bonnie. 'You wouldn't know they were robots?'

'Well,' said Sylvia, 'maybe you'd know, but they are uncannily lifelike, like the Stepford Wives.'

'Presumably they can only do what they've been programmed to do?' said Bonnie.

'I imagine so,' said Sylvia.

'You couldn't order them to kill all humans.'

'You could try, but I doubt they'd do it,' said Sylvia. 'You could probably order a sandwich.'

'You can do that at an Ibis as well,' said Bonnie. 'There's a twenty-four-hour snack service.'

'Have you seen the Ancient Egyptian images,' asked Sylvia, 'of a man with the head of an ibis, writing? It was the Egyptians,' she added, 'who reared ibises specifically for sacrificial purposes.'

'And Comfort Inns,' said Bonnie. 'I would try them too.'

'Who do you go on holiday with?' asked Sylvia.

'I used to go with my mum and dad,' said Bonnie, 'but eventually they decided it was time I started going away with my friends. I haven't been on holiday for a while. I can't really afford it anyway.'

'I haven't been away for years,' said Sylvia. 'We should go somewhere together. We could go to Devon.'

'That would be really nice,' said Bonnie, turning and looking at Sylvia as they walked along. 'I'd really like that. There's an Ibis in Devon.'

'Leave it with me,' said Sylvia. 'I'll look into it.'

'I'd need a ground-floor room,' said Bonnie.

They were almost home when Bonnie suddenly said, 'Oh, I completely forgot that you'd met Mum before. You told me you used to know her. I would have mentioned it to her if I'd thought. You didn't say anything about it in the restaurant. And I don't think she recognised you.'

'No,' said Sylvia. 'I don't think she did.'

They turned onto their street, and Bonnie thought that her mother might not like the idea of her walking the length of Slash Lane in the dark, but at least, she thought, as she passed beneath the broken street lamps, she was with a friend.

II

MY GRANDMOTHER WAS born in the same year as the behaviourist B. F. Skinner. My grandmother used to threaten to put me in a box and keep me there until I learned to behave. This, she said, was how Skinner had trained his daughter. Apparently, this is a myth—Skinner's "baby box" was more like "an upgraded playpen" with a "thermostatically controlled environment" and padded corners (Slater, *Opening Skinner's Box: Great Psychological Experiments of the Twentieth Century*)—but I didn't know this at the time. My grandmother told me that she would get my grandfather to build the box. He had a workshed and had built a bird table and I knew that he could easily build a box. Whenever I misbehaved, my grandmother would tell my grandfather to go to the workshed and get on with constructing the box, and he would go, and I would try very hard to behave. "If you even think of getting up to anything, Sylvia," my grandmother would say, "I will be the first to know about it." Even if I left the room, she would call after me, "I've got my eye on you!"

I tried to do helpful things, like dusting the mantelpiece or washing up the teacups, but my grandmother did not like me to do it. "You'll do it all wrong," she would say, or, "You'll break something. I know what you're like." If my mother let me carry my own glass to the table, my grandmother would say to me, "You're going to drop it," and when I did, and while I stared down at the smashed glass at my feet, my grandmother would say, "I knew you would."

My mother read child development manuals, turning back the corners of the pages here and there: "Failures of every sort are usually traceable not to a lack of ability, not to bad luck . . . but to a tendency in the subject to maintain the condition in which he has learned to feel at home . . . One of the deepest impulses in the very social human animal is to do what he perceives is expected of him" (Liedloff, *The Continuum Concept*). My mother asked my grandmother not to talk to me that way. "If you say she's going to drop it, she will," said my mother, walking in with the dustpan and brush.

"So she dropped it *because* I warned her not to?" said my grandmother, raising one thin, scathing eyebrow. "Get away from that glass," she said to me. "You're going to cut yourself."

"You didn't warn her *not* to drop the glass," said my mother. "You told her she *would* drop it. But Jean Liedloff says it's the same either way. Whether you tell her, 'You'll drop it,' or whether you tell her, 'Don't drop it,' what she hears is your expectation that she will drop it, and so she does, she complies."

"I didn't *tell* her to drop it," replied my grandmother. "I didn't *make* her drop it."

"On some level," said my mother, "you did." She bent down and picked up the big pieces of glass, holding them in her cupped hand.

"You'll cut yourself," said my grandmother. My mother pursed her lips and carried the big pieces into the kitchen, where I heard the sound of the glass being wrapped up in newspaper, the package going into the bin, a cupboard being opened. When she came back into the room, my mother made no reference to the fresh plaster I saw on her finger. She picked up the dustpan and brush and began to clear up the smaller pieces of broken glass.

"I hear *you* say such things," countered my grandmother. "When she isn't careful on the road, you tell her, 'One of these days, a car is going to knock you down.' When she walks on the wall, you tell her, 'You're going to fall.' Will you make these things happen just by saying them?"

My mother, sweeping, said, "Jean Liedloff says I shouldn't say things like that. She says that if we say to a child, 'Watch out, you'll hurt yourself,' the child, quite unconsciously, endeavours to do so, as if following an order. If we say, 'One of these days, a car is going to knock you down,' the child understands that one day that is going to happen, as if they have been promised something. She mentions a child who got over a fence and into a swimming pool and drowned *because* he was warned so often about that happening. He drowned because he was expected to."

My grandmother made a dismissive noise and went outside, into the garden, where my grandfather was working in the shed at the end of the path. My mother went back into the kitchen with the dustpan and brush and I heard her tipping all those little broken bits into the bin. I stayed where I was. Was I more likely, I wondered, to drop a glass that I was carrying, or knock over the ornaments on the mantelpiece, or break the teacups in the sink, if I was told I would, or if I was told not to? I stood still, in socks on the living room's swept-clean floorboards, looking for the glint of a stray shard.

At school, in the sixth form, I began reading Freud who, in explaining a dream of his, revealed that when he was born, an old peasant-woman prophesied to his mother that she had brought a great man into the world. I was studying psychology at the time, and came across Rosenthal and Jacobson and the elementary schoolchildren who were given a fake assessment, after which a randomly chosen group of these children was reported to the teachers to be showing signs of imminent intellectual blooming. This so influenced expectations regarding the children's abilities that those assigned to the "spurting" group actually did spurt, finishing up with higher IQs. And what about the other ones, I wondered, the ones who did not "spurt": how were they doing now? Thus, I discovered "the Golem effect", in which low expectations cause poor performance in subjects, the observation of which confirms and reinforces low expectations, and so on. I read some of Merton's work: his demonstration of how a "prophecy of collapse led to its own fulfillment". In a footnote, Merton had added: "Counterpart of the self-fulfilling prophecy is the 'suicidal prophecy' which so alters human behavior from what would have been its course had the prophecy not been made, that it *fails* to be borne out" (Merton, *Social Theory and Social Structure*). I wondered about the influence of personality type on the outcome of a prophecy, on whether the prophecy proves to be self-fulfilling or suicidal. One pupil is told that she is "going nowhere" and becomes stuck on this path that has been described for her, and she does indeed go nowhere. On the other hand, there have been children whose school reports have called them "hopeless" and said that they were "on the road to failure", whose junior school teachers wrote that, "This boy will never get anywhere in life" and, "He cannot be trusted to behave himself anywhere", and these children—John Lennon MBE, Eric Morecambe OBE and Sir Winston Churchill—have gone on to be exceptionally successful in life (Hurley, *Could Do Better: School Reports of the Great and the Good*). Some people's internal drives are no doubt stronger than the external factors acting upon them, and some people's drives must be weaker, or at least their drives are different. Perhaps, for some people, the prophecy itself is irrelevant, while for others it is clearly influential. There is also the question of the point at which we might say that a narrative is complete, that it has reached its conclusion. We do not leave the story of Oedipus when he sets out for Thebes, resisting the prophecy that has been explained to him by the oracle. We see what happens next, and in the end he cannot help himself. A prophecy that has not come true today might still come true tomorrow, or in twenty years' time, or within the hour. The bubble might yet burst.

Having become interested in behaviourism, conditioning, and stimulus-response psychology, I begged my parents for a kitten, and when we got one I began to conduct behavioural experiments. In the acquisition stage of its conditioning, the kitten learnt to respond to my whistling at feeding time. I then tested to see how long it would take for the kitten to unlearn that association, to stop running to its empty bowl when I whistled. These were the extinction trials. It never did unlearn the response, although I suppose at some point I just abandoned the experiment. Ideally, I wanted to recreate the experiments which I had read about in my textbook, but I did not know how to go about making Pavlov's one-way glass panel, or "an enclosed compartment [in which a subject could be] periodically subjected to electric shock (by electrifying the floor)" (Atkinson *et al*, *Introduction to Psychology*). I conducted experiments on my little brother. I would tell him, "Come here, I've got a present for you," and sometimes, when he came to me, I would give him some little gift, and sometimes I would pinch him. I recorded the data as a graph.

I read about LeShan, who experimented with sleep learning in relation to nail biting. Hundreds of times a night, for weeks, he played to a number of sleeping boys the phrase, "My fingernails are terribly bitter." He claimed some success (although his phonograph eventually broke, requiring him personally to stand in the room at night repeating the phrase while the boys slept). And I read about Cameron, who was similarly interested in mind control techniques and who tried to reprogramme his bedbound subjects' brains, playing taped messages to them through headphones for hours each day, day after day, for months. He is reported to have had some success with the message, "When you see a piece of paper, you want to pick it up." I also read up on Skinner, who believed that human free will is an illusion. Around 30 years ago psychologist Benjamin Libet discovered that if you ask people to make voluntary movements, their brains initiate the movement before they become consciously aware of any intention to move. Other experiments have since been performed along similar lines, leading many neuroscientists to conclude that free will is an illusion.

Fascinated by the potential of sleep learning and mind control, I also developed a curiosity about hypnosis, and specifically posthypnotic suggestion in which a suggestion made to a hypnotised subject is "activated" in the posthypnotic "waking" state, perhaps when a cue is given. I attempted to hypnotise my brother. However, he was uncooperative, despite me trying a very wide range of both traditional and innovative methods. I saw hypnosis done on stage, subjects convinced that they were Madonna, or that they were playing a trumpet when no trumpet was there, or that their chair was burning hot. I was most intrigued by the idea of *negative* hallucination, where the subject will fail to see what is right there in front of them. In the subject's imagination, the hypnotist's clothes disappear, or their own clothes disappear. The trick gets a big laugh and everyone claps and the subjects go back to their seats.

My other interest was drama. Our school had a good drama department and I got involved in set design. I was fascinated by the ability of a neutral performance space to become a desert or a hotel room via the dressing of the space with papier mâché cacti or a bed and maybe a picture on the wall. It was not really the set design that was important: it was that we—the performers and the audience—all agreed to believe that the performance space was, at this moment, a desert or a hotel room.

I attached myself to the drama department at university as well, taking classes in video production, which introduced me to the editing suite. Meanwhile, I was majoring in psychology, and saw a recording of the 1962 film of Stanley Milgram's Obedience experiment, in which everyone was playing a role, was part of the act, except for the naive subject. I discovered the work of James Vicary, and began to take an interest in the possibility of subliminal messaging.

It was around that time that I had my first run-in with the university, receiving my first warning. In my defence, I cited Milgram, and Watson, and others who had not been hampered by impossible-to-know long-term effects on their subjects. All sorts of things which used to be allowed in experimental psychology are unfortunately no longer permitted, formally.

12

'I THOUGHT WE were going to stay in an Ibis,' said Bonnie, switching on the kettle. 'Or a Comfort Inn if there is one.'

'No,' said Sylvia. 'This is better. We're going to Seaton, because that's where your story is set.'

'It's set in Sea*town*,' said Bonnie, 'a fictional Seatown.'

'It's obviously Seaton,' said Sylvia. '*I* can see that, even if you can't.'

'And either way,' said Bonnie, 'why are we going there?'

'If you go there, you might find out how your story ends,' said Sylvia.

'Fiona thinks it's strange that I'm going on holiday with you,' said Bonnie.

'Does she?' said Sylvia. 'Why's that?'

'You're my landlady,' said Bonnie.

'I don't see what's so strange about it,' said Sylvia. 'We'll be one another's travelling companions, like in *Rebecca*: I'll be Mrs Van Hopper and you'll be my young lady companion on the Côte d'Azur.'

'I don't think I have a name, do I?' said Bonnie.

'Oh, you have one,' said Sylvia. 'We just don't know what it is. We know it's something unusual and hard to spell.'

'And I remember that she doesn't much like Monte Carlo,' said Bonnie. 'She finds it artificial.'

'Well,' said Sylvia. 'It is what it is.'

'And it doesn't end well, does it?' said Bonnie. 'It ends with everything ablaze.' It ended with the smell of ash mixed with the salt wind from the sea.

'Well, that's not Mrs Van Hopper's fault,' said Sylvia.

'My character seems to think it might be. If it wasn't for Mrs Van Hopper, I'd never have become Mrs de Winter,' said Bonnie. 'You know,' she added, 'I know very little about you. You know a lot more about me.'

'I'll see if I can get us rooms above the Hook and Parrot,' said Sylvia.

'I don't think they do rooms,' said Bonnie.

'But it's in your story,' said Sylvia. 'That's where Susan stays.'

'I think there *are* rooms upstairs,' said Bonnie, 'but not for people to stay in. I think it's just a pub.'

'So that's not where you stayed when you went there as a child?'

'No,' said Bonnie. 'We stayed in a caravan park.'

'Well,' said Sylvia. 'Maybe they do rooms now.'

'I need to be on the ground floor,' said Bonnie.

'Don't worry about that,' said Sylvia. 'Leave it to me. Are you waiting for this cup of tea to make itself?'

While Bonnie made the teas, Sylvia went ahead to the lounge. When Bonnie came through, Sylvia was standing near the desk, browsing through a small pile of new library books.

'Is this your holiday reading?' she asked. '*Heart of Darkness. The Sheltering Sky.* I can imagine you reading these in your room at the Ibis, journeying up the Congo and trekking into the North African desert while you're lying on your bed.'

'I thought we weren't staying in an Ibis?' said Bonnie.

'No,' said Sylvia. 'No, we're not.' She took her cup of tea and drank it while she browsed through a Rough Guide volume that Bonnie had read, in which women braved Taliban-occupied Afghanistan; and Antarctica, where blinking for too long caused your eyes to freeze shut; and countries where leeches found their way onto your body, onto any and every part of you, even your privates, tiny ones worming unseen through your clothes; and where earthquakes parted the ground beneath you, the road you'd been travelling on, leaving you stranded.

'I was wondering about getting into travel writing,' said Bonnie, and Sylvia laughed. 'I was going to try some travel writing when I stayed in that Ibis. I was going to write about a museum I'd planned to go to, but I went on the wrong day and it was closed, so I just got a taxi back to the hotel.'

Sylvia smiled and said, 'Have you written any more of your story?'

'No,' said Bonnie. 'I was thinking of seeing if I could get anything done this weekend.'

'Put more detail into it,' said Sylvia. 'I want to be able to picture what everything looks like. What's the wallpaper like in the bedroom? What's the picture on the wall? Whereabouts in the room is the bed? You had a blanket in the first part, but now it's a duvet. And what colour is it?'

'Oh,' said Bonnie. 'Yellow?'

Sylvia finished her tea. 'Well,' she said, 'I'll leave you to it, and when you've written it I'd like to read it.'

'Maybe you can read it while we're in Seaton,' said Bonnie.

'No,' said Sylvia, 'before that. I'll pop round again in a week.' She looked at the boxes from under the stairs. 'I'll take some of this away with me as well.' She handed Bonnie her empty cup and picked up the cool box and another box that contained assorted bits and bobs. 'See if you can find a teapot,' she said, nodding to the other boxes. 'It makes a better cup of tea.'

III

13

SUSAN DREAMT THAT she was in a hotel, walking back to her room, but she could not get her eyes to open properly; she could not hold them open long enough to read the numbers on the bedroom doors. And so she wandered up and down the corridor, unable to find her room.

Waking, she found that she was not in fact walking endlessly in a corridor but lying in her bed, which was in the corner furthest from the door. She liked that her bed was in the corner; she liked to go to sleep against a wall, although she always found that she rolled to the opposite side, the side that was not against a wall, during the night. She still remembered the childhood bump of tumbling out of bed.

The sun was shining on the floral wallpaper, and Susan turned towards the window and saw the unbroken blue sky.

Her foot had gone to sleep, and she did not wait long enough before standing. The foot, as if boneless, dragged lamely on the patterned carpet as she went towards the window. She inspected the glass for marks where the paper must have been stuck to it in the night, but there was nothing, no residue. She opened the window wide and looked down at the pavement below, but saw no square of paper that might have been on the outside of the window before coming unstuck and dropping down. Perhaps what she had seen against the window in the night had just been something blown against the glass and then blown away again, or perhaps it had, in fact, somehow, been a reflection of something, perhaps a reflection of the picture after all, which was a still life, apples in a bowl, by Cézanne, whose walls slid, whose chairs bent, whose cloths curled like burning paper, whose perspective was distorted and who took liberties with reality.

Or perhaps she had not really seen it at all; perhaps she had only dreamt it.

She lit a cigarette. When she inhaled, the tip of her cigarette glowed orange like a dashboard warning light. She leaned over the sill to blow out smoke rings, which floated up, dispersing. They looked like cartoon wailing or surprise: o O O. She took a final puff, dropped the butt and watched it spark on the slabs. A cyclist on the pavement steered around it.

Susan put on yesterday's clothes. She needed to go to the launderette, but she would not go today because she was working behind the bar.

The pub was always quiet during the week. Joe would probably come in; he usually spent his lunch hour in the Hook. Susan had been on one date with Joe. It had gone well, she thought, although he had been too busy for a second date; and then at some point, without anything having been said, it became clear to her that it was not going to happen, which was fine. They were friends now; she pulled his pints.

Towards noon, Susan took out her powder compact and retouched her make-up. At two o'clock, Joe walked through the door. He came to the bar and Susan served him. 'I had the strangest night,' she said, putting the pint down on the bar in front of him. 'Well, it started yesterday really. I'd just woken up, and I saw a piece of paper near the door, like a message that had been pushed underneath, but when I went to look at it, it was blank, or I thought it was, but there might have been something on it that I couldn't quite make out. And then last night I woke up and you know how I've got no curtains?'

Joe did not respond. His attention was on a woman at the far end of the bar. She looked like a mannequin, made out of pale pink plastic or fibreglass. The man she was with leaned forward to kiss her, and she let him but she kept her eyes open while he did it. Her false eyelashes looked like a spider's legs on her brow bone and the top of her cheek, which gave Susan the shivers, thinking about spiders crawling across your face in the night, and swallowing them in your sleep—she had read that somewhere, that we swallow eight spiders a year in our sleep. Perhaps it was not even true but now she was scared of the thought anyway and imagined spiders creeping out of their hidey-holes and onto her face the moment she fell asleep. She had even mentioned this to Joe, and he had told her that he would like to get hold of a plastic spider and put it on her face while she was sleeping, to scare the crap out of her when she woke up.

Susan, who had been going on with her story of the night before, stopped dead in the middle of her sentence. Was it Joe, playing tricks on her? He could have got hold of her keys, got them copied. With a set of keys, he could let himself in and out of the pub, in and out of her room while she slept.

Joe reached out and touched Susan's frown line with the tip of his forefinger. This was something he did: if she had been talking for too long, he pretended to switch her off. Now, as if she were a machine whose screen had frozen mid-task, with his fingertip pressed into her flesh, against the bone of her forehead, he rebooted her: 'Beep,' he said.

'Have you been in my room?' said Susan.

'You know I have,' said Joe, grinning.

'No, I mean, have you been in my room when I've been asleep?'

'Well, yes,' said Joe.

'Yes, but I mean, without me knowing you were there?'

Joe raised an eyebrow.

'I've been finding all these notes,' said Susan, 'slipped under my door and stuck to my window.'

Joe shrugged. 'They're not from me. Did you think they were from me? Why would I be sticking notes onto your f***ing window? What do they say, these notes?'

'I'm not sure they say anything. But I think they might say, "JUMP".'

Joe gave her a look, the same look he'd given her when she'd asked him if he wanted to come to her parents' at Christmas. 'You think someone's slipping you notes that tell you to jump, but you're not sure?'

'The notes appear when I'm asleep, and I can never quite make out what's written on them.'

'Look, if you've been dreaming that messages are telling you to jump, well, don't. Don't jump out of the window. OK?' He finished his pint and got up to leave. 'Back to the grindstone,' he said. 'No jumping out of the window, all right?' He walked to the door, and when he got there he turned and said again, as he disappeared through the doorway, 'Don't jump.'

The mannequin woman and her partner left too, leaving Susan alone in the bar. She helped herself to a drink and looked through the local paper for the quick crossword puzzle. She wrote her answers lightly in pencil, and doodled while she thought.

The radio was on, as it always was. It was tuned to a local station that played love songs and adverts. Susan turned the dial and found a poet talking about how stealing something changes it. 'You want it,' he said, 'you decide to take it, but now that it's in your hands suddenly it's different, it automatically begins to reshape into something else.' It made Susan think of some sweets that she had once tried to steal. She had selected a packet and tucked it up her sleeve. She had got as far as the doorway and was stepping outside when a hand grabbed her shoulder, and she had felt the sweets against the inside of her wrist; they were round and hard like pebbles inside the little scratchy packet that said 'WIN'.

'When William Burroughs and Brion Gysin were hanging out in the hotel on Rue Gît-le-Cœur and they were cutting up and rearranging newspapers,' continued the poet, 'they told people that they were trying to uncover the subliminal message hidden inside the original newspapers. They weren't thinking of themselves as like artists, they were more like cryptographers, right, 'cause after all, they're only showing you what's already there.'

Susan gave up on the crossword, turned the pencil over and rubbed out her answers and her doodles of eyes with lashes like spiders' legs. The landlady liked to do the crossword herself, and Susan was forbidden to touch it.

By the end of her shift, after hours of standing, Susan's legs were aching, as they always were. She went outside for some fresh air. It was nearly the end of October. Before the bonfire, there would be Halloween. She wondered if they did Halloween here. At home, in the village, there would be carved, lit pumpkins in the windows, and there would be witches and devils and monsters and ghouls in the streets, and fake police tape stretched across doorways, crime scene tape saying 'DO NOT ENTER', 'HAUNTED HOUSE— DO NOT ENTER', and on doorsteps and in entrances and hallways there would be bowls of sweets.

After finishing her cigarette, she went back inside, locked the door and went up to her room, where there was an air of mouldering, as if something was damp. She touched her hand to the carpet, and to the wallpaper, pressing down, but she could not find the source of the swampy smell.

She climbed into her bed, and went to sleep.

14

IT WAS THE longest day of the year, and Bonnie had spent it in the backyard, working on her story. Her laptop was plugged into a socket in the kitchen, the lead stretching out to the deckchair in which she was sitting. She had been working with the laptop balanced on her knees, and it had seemed inside out, to be sitting in the garden, typing; she had felt like she was in that short story of Raymond Carver's, 'Why Don't You Dance?', in which all the furniture is out in the yard, and a boy turns on the television set and sits down on the sofa to watch.

Now she had finished for the day. She had closed her laptop and propped it against the side of the deckchair. *She climbed into her bed, and went to sleep.* Bonnie wondered if that was a reasonable place to stop. She felt as if half the scenes in her story ended with Susan going back to sleep, as if there were some force in the narrative relentlessly drawing Susan to her bed; as if, in daylight, Susan was only ever marking time until she could go back to her bed and sleep; as if day was only ever leading to night, although of course it was.

In Bonnie's own backyard, afternoon had become evening. She was just wondering what to do with herself when Sylvia came through the passageway. 'Oh, Bonnie!' said Sylvia, when she saw Bonnie sitting there. 'Don't you normally have a shift now? Why aren't you at work?'

'I didn't feel like going in,' said Bonnie, glancing at her watch. She ought to have been at the Lab an hour ago.

Sylvia noticed the laptop leaning against Bonnie's deck-chair. 'Have you written more of your story?' she asked.

'A little bit more,' said Bonnie. 'It's still not finished.'

'When can I read it?' asked Sylvia.

'When it's finished,' said Bonnie. This was what she had said after writing the previous installment, and Sylvia had responded by badgering Bonnie until she handed the pages over to her after all. Bonnie half-expected a rerun of the episode now.

Sylvia gave her a smile. 'All right,' she said. She turned to look at the planters. The clematis and the wisteria were not doing well. 'What have you done to the climbers?' she asked.

'Nothing,' said Bonnie.

'I'll give them some water,' said Sylvia, moving towards the back door. 'May I use the kitchen?'

'Of course,' said Bonnie.

Sylvia went inside and turned on the tap. After the water had been running for a little while, it occurred to Bonnie that if Sylvia was looking around for a jug, there wasn't one. She was about to get up and go inside when the tap was turned off and Sylvia came out carrying the kettle. She watered the climbers, and said to Bonnie, 'Have you remembered to print out your story?'

'I can't at the moment,' said Bonnie. 'My printer's not working. Or at least it isn't recognising my laptop.'

'Ah,' said Sylvia, emptying the kettle into the last of the planters.

'Shall we have a cup of tea?' asked Bonnie, preparing to move.

'I can't stop,' said Sylvia. 'I've got things to do.' She returned the kettle to the kitchen. 'I've sorted out the accommodation for our holiday. I was going to leave you a note. I've got us rooms above the Hook and Parrot.'

'Have you?' said Bonnie. 'I didn't think they did rooms.'

'They do now,' said Sylvia.

'I really need a ground-floor room,' said Bonnie.

'You need to be in a room above the Hook and Parrot,' said Sylvia, 'because that's where Susan stays.'

'I don't actually say it's the Hook and Parrot,' said Bonnie, 'or that it's Seaton.'

'But it is,' said Sylvia, 'really.' She gave her climbers one last disappointed look. 'We'll get that story of yours finished,' she added, and she disappeared down the passageway again.

The sinking sun shone through the bare trellis, leaving the backyard crosshatched with bars of shadow, behind which Bonnie sat for a little while longer, before going inside.

She ate some leftovers, then got into bed and began reading *Rebecca* again, much of which she had forgotten. She remembered the stark ending, but not how it came about.

From her bed, through the gap in the curtains, Bonnie could see the sky, in which, at eleven o'clock, there was still some light. It was not quite like daylight—it was not a sun-in-the-sky kind of light, or it was at least as if a raincloud were covering the sun—but the sky was still a kind of blue. The street lamps were on, though, as well. Even an hour later, there was still a dusky light in the sky, as if someone had forgotten to bring the dimmer switch all the way down.

While she was reading, she drifted off, and when she opened her eyes again she did not know how much time had passed. The starlit sky was cornflower blue. At three-something a.m., when the night still did not seem really to have got started, the birds began singing. It was as if whoever was in charge of the lighting desk and the sound desk in the control booth had made a mistake, had fallen asleep on the job. Bonnie dozed again, and when she woke, the sun was shining in between the drawn curtains. It was the morning after the longest day—it was downhill now, her grandmother would have said, all the way to winter.

15

OVER THE NEXT few weeks, Bonnie saw very little of Sylvia, so little that she started to think that something might be up, that perhaps she had completely misread Sylvia. 'I'm getting paranoid!' Bonnie said to Fiona. 'She hardly ever comes round now, and when I do see her she's dashing off somewhere. If she's gone off the idea of us going away together, maybe you and I could do something instead.'

''Fraid not,' said Fiona. 'I've already made plans.'

'Where are you going?' asked Bonnie.

'I'm not sure yet,' said Fiona. 'But I am going.'

The Lab was not a place where anyone stayed for long. Bonnie was well aware that Fiona hated the place, and Mr Carr. She asked Fiona how long she was going to stay there for, but Fiona would not say just when she would leave or what plans she had made.

'How about you?' asked Fiona.

'I'll probably stay,' said Bonnie, although she disliked it too.

On a Friday in July, a few days before Bonnie was due to go on holiday with Sylvia, Bonnie watched a matinee showing of a science fiction film before heading for her evening job. As she passed the 'CUNT' bench, on which two women were sitting, talking, one of them said, 'Just quit.'

Bonnie bought a chocolate bar and ate it while she walked to the Lab. Halfway down a quiet side street, she became aware of two or more men, wearing dark clothes, baseball caps and shades, following some distance behind her. They were like something escaped from the film she had just seen, and she walked a little faster. When she looked back over her shoulder, the men had gone.

Fiona was already in the staff room. She was sitting down while Mr Carr stood over her, with his shirt open, showing off the tattoo on his chest. When Bonnie came into the room, Mr Carr rebuttoned his shirt, although Bonnie caught sight of the legend, or part of it, tattooed across his broad chest: I am the master. It reminded Bonnie of her student housemate's recitation: 'I am the master of my fate.' It was from an old poem. That was probably what Mr Carr's tattoo said as well: I am the master of my fate. Perhaps they were, she thought; or perhaps they were like Number Six in *The Prisoner*, trapped in the Village and insisting, 'I am a free man!'

'Go on, then,' he said to the two of them. 'Get to work.'

Bonnie cleaned her corridors, and was on her way back to the staff room when she saw Fiona coming from the store room. She could see that Fiona had already collected her belongings, and as they neared one another, Fiona, with a spring in her step, said, 'I won't see you on Monday.'

'No,' said Bonnie. As far as she knew, she was still going on holiday. 'But I'll be back at the end of the week. I'll see you then.'

'No,' said Fiona, 'I won't see you again.'

'Are you quitting?' asked Bonnie.

'I guess so,' said Fiona, passing her by with a grin, without stopping, turning her head to say, 'I have to go. My friends are waiting for me.'

Bonnie had to go to the staff room to pick up her jacket and her bag. She was not looking forward to seeing Mr Carr. She had dragged her feet over asking for time off for her holiday. Mr Carr did not like it when people asked for time off, and Bonnie had continually failed to start the conversation, until eventually it had got too late to ask. If he saw her, he would say to her, 'See you on Monday, don't be late,' and Bonnie would have to mumble something in reply. Under her breath, she said, 'Please, please, please.'

Mr Carr was not in the staff room. Bonnie collected her things and headed towards the gate. She would still have to face him when she got back. Although, in fact, she had started to think about quitting. She would make that decision later though. Right now, she needed to do her packing, and nothing was clean. She had been meaning to go to the launderette but she had not got around to it.

As she left the complex, she half-expected the men in black, the men in dark glasses, to be there, waiting, but she did not see them.

She put in her earphones. She had abandoned the language course. Instead, she half-listened to music as she wandered home.

She passed a gym with posters in the windows that said 'JOIN NOW'. She had been a member of this gym, despite the fact that she had never really been able to afford the fee. She had only ever been inside once, to use the swimming pool, and although she had always meant to go back, somehow it had never happened. She had already signed their forms though—they had her bank details—and so her membership money had been direct-debited from her bank account at the start of each month for the rest of the year.

She ought to swim more though, she thought; she ought to get fit. She ought to join again.

For supper, Bonnie worked her way through a family pack of crisps. She opened up her laptop and discovered that the connection to her printer was working again. The elves, her grandmother would have said, had been working their magic. As a child, Bonnie had been troubled by the thought of these elves who let themselves into people's private rooms and worked their strange magic, fixed their shoes in the middle of the night, and then left again without being seen, although you knew that they had been there.

She printed out the latest part of her story and put it away in the desk drawer with the rest. She finished the crisps and left her laptop to go to sleep. 'But what happens next?' she said to herself. Where could she go from where she was? And where *was* she? Susan suspected Joe of coming into her room while she was sleeping, but that was not likely to be the case, reckoned Bonnie as she brushed her teeth. And Susan had been thinking about Halloween coming, thought Bonnie as she put on her nightie, or about whether or not it would be coming to the seaside. And then she climbed into her bed, and went to sleep.

16

WAKING LATE ON the Saturday morning, it occurred to Bonnie that she had not told her parents that she was going away. They would want to know, she thought. She would not mention, though, that she was thinking of quitting her job. She would have to not say that. *Do not say that*, she told herself.

The landline was in her bedroom; her telephone was on the bedside table. She would be able to make or take an emergency call in the middle of the night without leaving her bed. She had an old-fashioned style of telephone, the type with a dial on the front and the receiver in a cradle. Her mother had worried that it would take too long for her to dial 999, but Bonnie had explained that the dial was just for show, that it was really a push-button model. It had been sold as a novelty telephone, which made it sound as if it would not actually work, as if it were just a prop. It was black, and whenever she used it, she felt as if she were a femme fatale in a Hitchcock film, although she mainly used it to call her mother, or to call for pizza.

She phoned home and spoke to her father, who said, 'I'll put your mother on.'

When her mother came on the line, Bonnie said to her, 'I forgot to tell you that I'm going away on Monday. I'm going to the seaside with Sylvia for a few days.'

'Who's Sylvia?' asked her mother.

'My landlady,' said Bonnie. 'You met her at my birthday meal.'

'Why are you going away with your landlady?' asked her mother.

'She suggested it,' said Bonnie, 'and I said yes. We're going to Devon.'

'What about your job?' asked her mother. 'Have they given you time off?'

'Not really,' said Bonnie. 'But I was thinking of quitting anyway.'

'Oh Bonnie,' said her mother. 'You're going to quit, again? Listen . . . Are you listening?'

Half an hour after putting the phone down, Bonnie's mother was at the back door. She had brought Bonnie's father along too.

'Talk to her,' said Bonnie's mother.

Bonnie's father said to Bonnie, 'You haven't got an ounce of sense.' He positioned himself in the doorway that led from the kitchen to the lounge, leaning against the frame.

Bonnie's mother had also brought along a shopping bag full of food, as well as her apron and recipes, and clean plates and cutlery. 'Because you don't eat properly,' she said, unpacking everything onto the kitchen counter. When Bonnie had still been living at home, she had tried every now and again to make the family meals, but her efforts had never gone right. She did not have the knack of getting everything onto the plates at the same time, so something was always going cold, while something else was still half-raw or half-frozen. Her father would eye with great suspicion the dishes that she made. Her mother would at least try things before saying that she was not all that hungry. Bonnie's attempts had invariably ended with a trip to the fish and chip shop.

While Bonnie's mother was preparing the lunch, Sylvia came into the backyard, looked in through the kitchen window and opened the door.

'Perhaps Sylvia can talk some sense into you,' said Bonnie's mother, turning to Sylvia to say, 'She's thinking of quitting her job.'

'Is she?' said Sylvia, coming into the kitchen and closing the door behind her, and Bonnie felt as if she were at the centre of some kind of intervention.

'I'm making lunch,' said Bonnie's mother to Sylvia. 'You'll stay, won't you?'

'I'm afraid I can't,' said Sylvia. 'I just popped by to speak to Bonnie. I didn't realise she had visitors.'

'Well, have a drink at least. Bonnie, nobody has a drink.'

Bonnie made a cup of tea for her father, but Sylvia declined. 'I can't stay long,' she said. 'I just want a word.'

Bonnie took her father and Sylvia through to the lounge. It was the weekend of the Wimbledon finals, and Saturday's match was due to start. Bonnie asked her father if he wanted to watch it. 'Don't bother,' he said. 'It's only the ladies playing this afternoon.' He tried his tea, pulled a face, and said, 'So, you're going down to Devon on Monday, are you?'

'Yes,' said Bonnie.

Her father looked at Sylvia and said to her, 'I hope you're doing the driving. Don't let that one behind the wheel!' He pointed at Bonnie. 'If you drive,' he said to Bonnie, 'you'll crash! Or else clear the roads first,' and he put a hand up to his mouth, making it into a megaphone through which he bellowed, 'Clear the roads!' He sat back, laughing.

Bonnie's mother came in, brushing her hands off on the front of her apron, which said, 'I'M THE BOSS!' She said to Bonnie's father, 'Have you spoken to her about quitting her job?'

'I'm sure they'll struggle on without her,' said Bonnie's father.

'That's not what I meant. I mean she's talking about *quitting*, *again*, and with nothing lined up, nothing to go to.'

Bonnie remembered then to say to her mother, 'Sylvia said you used to know each other, when I was little.'

'I thought you looked familiar,' said Bonnie's mother, but at the same time she was clearly struggling to place Sylvia.

Bonnie said to Sylvia, 'How did you say you knew Mum?'

'Do you know,' said Sylvia, 'I wonder if I made a mistake about that?'

'No,' said Bonnie's mother, looking hard at Sylvia. 'You do look familiar. But I can't think . . . Which school did you go to?'

Twenty questions later, Bonnie's mother was still none the wiser, and she had to go back to the kitchen to see to the meal.

'She's failed her test three times,' said Bonnie's father to Sylvia. '*Three times*.' He held up three fingers.

'I passed in the end,' said Bonnie.

'They must have been desperate to see the back of you,' said her father.

'Shall we watch the tennis?' said Bonnie, but her father had the remote control.

'Where's your lavatory?' he asked, and when Bonnie directed him through the kitchen, he took the remote control with him.

Now that they were alone, Sylvia turned to Bonnie and said, 'Are you all set for Monday?'

'Pretty much,' said Bonnie, who had not actually started packing but planned to do so first thing in the morning, after visiting the launderette.

'Have you managed to print out that new section of your Seatown story yet?'

'I have,' said Bonnie. 'The printer's working again.'

'Oh good,' said Sylvia. 'And have you written any more?'

'No,' said Bonnie. 'I was going to think about it last night, but I fell asleep instead.'

'All right,' said Sylvia, 'well, give me what you've written and then I can read it before we go. I can't wait to read it.'

'I'd rather not,' said Bonnie. 'Not just yet.'

Her mother called from the kitchen, 'Bonnie! I think you've got mice!'

'Excuse me,' said Bonnie.

'Please,' said Sylvia, gesturing towards the kitchen door.

Bonnie left the room, saying to her mother, 'I wondered if I had. I thought I'd heard something scratching.'

When Bonnie returned to the lounge, Sylvia said, 'I'd better go, dear.'

'It looks as if some mice got in,' said Bonnie.

'All right,' said Sylvia, as she picked her way past the road signs' metal legs. 'Let me know if you see them.' As she passed through the kitchen, Sylvia peered into the pot that was bubbling away on the stove. 'That smells delicious,' she said.

'The recipe's just there,' said Bonnie's mother, nodding towards it while she stirred. 'If you give me a minute, I'll copy it out for you.'

'There's no need,' said Sylvia, who had her phone in her hand and was angling the screen over the page of text. She took a photo. 'Got it,' she said.

'I'm sure I do know you,' said Bonnie's mother. 'I just can't think *how*. Who's your dentist?'

'I really do have to go,' said Sylvia, moving towards the back door. 'I must finish my packing. Ah!' she exclaimed, looking at the table with folding legs, which had come out from under the stairs and was now getting in the way in the kitchen. 'I'll take this off your hands,' she said, picking it up. It was lightweight but long, and Bonnie took one end of it and helped Sylvia to steer the table through the doorway and into the passageway. Bonnie felt like someone in a gag trying to get a ladder through a series of doorways, someone like Stan Laurel, who was always in some kind of trouble, some kind of foolish danger.

'All right,' said Sylvia, when they were standing on the pavement at the front of the house. 'This will do, you can put it down here.'

'I can bring it inside,' said Bonnie. 'I can help you get it up the stairs.' She had never seen inside Sylvia's part of the house.

'No,' said Sylvia, 'this is just fine. You can leave it with me now. You'd better be getting back—your dinner will be waiting for you.' She looked at her watch. 'I'm looking forward to our trip,' she added. 'I'll be here with the hire car at nine o'clock on Monday.'

When Bonnie got back to the kitchen, she found the light off, the stove off. Her mother called through from the lounge, 'We started without you.' Bonnie went through and her mother indicated the dish on the floor. 'Help yourself,' she said.

'I don't know how you can live like this,' said her father, balancing his full plate on his knees. 'Have you not got a table?'

'Funnily enough,' said Bonnie, 'I've just helped Sylvia take a table out of here.'

'Of course you have,' said her father.

They ate, and when they had all finished, Bonnie reached for her parents' empty plates. 'Let me take those,' she said.

'No,' said her mother. 'These are my good plates, I don't want you to break them.'

Bonnie's mother took the plates through to the kitchen and Bonnie said, 'Do we want afters?'

'What have you got?' asked her father.

Bonnie went and had a look in the fridge, and in the freezer compartment, and in her biscuit tin. 'I've got biscuits,' she said.

'What sort of biscuits?' asked her father.

'Broken,' said Bonnie. 'I got a kilogram.'

'I think we'll just go,' said her mother, who had washed up the plates and was packing them away, along with everything else that she had brought with her.

Bonnie walked her parents to their car. Bonnie's mother, after getting in and closing her door, wound down her window to say, 'Have a good trip!' and Bonnie's father, behind the wheel, shouted up at Sylvia's flat, 'Don't let her drive!' There was no sign of Sylvia though; there were no lights on.

Bonnie returned to the flat, to the lounge, where she switched on the television and sat and watched the tennis.

She always meant to follow Wimbledon, but somehow she never did, not all the way through to the end.

Her eyes followed the ball across the net, to and fro, like someone following a hypnotist's swinging pocket watch, to a background murmur of commentary. The game had a familiar lulling, rhythmic quality, but at the same time, underlying the tennis whites and the strawberries and cream, there was muscle and ferocity and steely-eyed tenacity.

The tennis finished while Bonnie was in the kitchen, boiling the kettle. She took her cup of tea back into the lounge and settled down again in front of the television to watch *Blade Runner*. She had seen the film before, but this, it turned out, was a different version: the Director's Cut. With one brief shot spliced into the middle of another scene and lasting only seconds, the Director's Cut introduced into the narrative a subtle but vital difference: Deckard's mental image of a unicorn running through the mist suggested that Deckard himself was a Replicant. It was unsettling, as if this must also have been true in the other version, as if this had been part of the narrative all along but without Bonnie ever having seen it, despite sitting through the whole film. Those few seconds made all the difference in the world, changing the meaning of Deckard finding the silver paper origami unicorn at the end of the film. How disturbing it would be, she thought, to discover, just like that, that you were not what you thought you were, that you were not real. And what had happened to her happy ending? In the Director's Cut, you no longer saw Deckard and Rachael driving off into the future. All that was just gone. 'That's not how it ends!' said Bonnie to the screen. She watched the closing credits, after which there was sometimes something more, something extra.

The screen faded to black.

Apparently there were other versions as well, but Bonnie was wary of seeing them.

She did not feel like going to bed just yet. She changed channels and watched an old silent film, the start of which she had already missed. Intertitles flashed up, like subliminal messaging for slower readers: 'What's the matter—afraid of Temptation?' Or like a fortune cookie message: 'The only way to get rid of a temptation is to yield to it'. The flickering text also reminded her of an installation that she had seen with her mother at Tate Liverpool: in a dark box of a room, she had sat on a bench facing a screen on which a short black and white film had looped, and in amongst the indistinct, ghostly images she had seen a phrase, 'THE DEATH OF TOI'. She had sat there watching the film of flickering light and shadows repeating, the words flashing up over and over again. She had been comfortable in there. It was not often she went to a gallery, and less often still that she understood a piece of modern art, but this, she felt, she did. She was talking about it as they left the gallery, and her mother said, 'I don't think that's what it said. Didn't you see the description?' Bonnie had not. The film, her mother explained, was a corrupted recreation of the final scene of the silent film of *Uncle Tom's Cabin*, and the caption was 'THE DEATH OF TOM'. Bonnie had seen something that was not really there, or rather, she had seen something that she was not meant to see. Now that she had seen it, though, she could not unsee it; she still saw it flashing up on the screen in her mind's eye as she walked with her mother up Water Street: 'THE DEATH OF TOI'.

The film that Bonnie was watching now came to an end: 'The End' appeared on the screen and Bonnie switched the television off. She made another cup of tea and took it to bed with her.

On Sunday afternoon, Bonnie went to the launderette. There was no one in there except for her, and the woman behind the counter who was in charge. There were machines going, but most people put their washing in and then left, and came back when their washing was done. Bonnie, though, had once put her washing into the machine and gone home and failed to return until after the launderette was closed. Now she stayed, to be on the safe side.

She put her washing into a machine and set it going. The woman behind the counter said, 'Hello, love,' and Bonnie turned around. The woman was not looking at her now; she was searching through a bag of laundry. Bonnie said hello but she might have said it too quietly to be heard; the woman did not look up. Bonnie sat down to wait. She had forgotten to bring a magazine. Her phone was in her pocket but she had neglected to charge it and the screen was dead.

The launderette had been given a fresh coat of paint; Bonnie could smell the fumes. The smell reminded her of ghosts. She had once—three times in fact—seen the ghost of Elvis Presley. She had been asleep in her bedroom, which was being painted at the time, the walls changing from a floral pattern to plain white, the blue flowers still showing through after the second coat, like the bell on Noddy's hat showing through the black paint on Adrian Mole's bedroom wall, the bell iterated dozens of times around the walls and still showing through coat after coat. Bonnie had woken up in the night and seen Elvis's ghost, which came forward out of a poster of him, which was still up on a wall that had not yet been painted, or else—she could not remember—the wall had already been painted and the poster had been put back up. The following night, the same thing happened, except that this time Elvis grew bigger, came closer. On the third night, he was bigger and closer still, a beautiful spectre looming over her. She did not tell her mother, who would have said that it was only the paint fumes. Bonnie knew that it was not just the paint fumes: she had seen it with her own eyes.

Bonnie watched her washing tumbling around inside the spinning machine. It was mesmeric. It made her feel sleepy.

The woman behind the counter said, 'You have to watch this programme they're showing at nine o'clock tonight on the BBC.'

'Oh,' said Bonnie. 'All right.'

The woman glanced up, and Bonnie realised that the woman was using a hands-free device; she was talking to somebody else.

'Sorry,' said Bonnie. 'You were talking to somebody else, weren't you?'

'Yes,' said the woman, but she had already looked away again and her reply might have been meant for the person on the other end of the phone.

When the washing machine came to a stop, Bonnie discovered that she had not brought enough money for the drier, and besides, the afternoon had disappeared and the launderette would be closing soon. She pulled her wet washing out of the machine into her Bag for Life and lugged it home. She draped her damp laundry over the washing line in the yard, and it hung there in the early evening shadows and in the dusk, barely drying at all, while Bonnie flicked between BBC channels, wondering which of the nine o'clock programmes was the right one.

17

MY SUBJECTS KNEW me as Dr Slythe. I had put an advertisement in the local paper, and a reasonable number of people had responded. I hired an upstairs room in a community centre on Waterside Close. The room was not one of those windowless boxes: it had a large window, which I opened, and I pinned a welcoming notice onto the door. I set up a television and a video player and put out a row of chairs for the participants. It was going to be, I thought, a little bit like one of those theatre shows where you think you're just in the audience but then, unexpectedly, you have become part of the performance, sometimes without even leaving your seat. The houselights go up and that's the signal, like the light which comes on before the meat powder is delivered into the dog's dish in Pavlov's experiment, or like the tone which the dog hears prior to receiving a shock in Rescorla's investigations, or in Maier and Seligman's experiments, which showed that dogs which have been taught through conditioning that they have no control over receiving shocks will, in the second stage of the experiment, when they do have a choice, make no attempt to avoid the shock.

I dressed the part, in a suit, navy blue, and I also had a white laboratory coat to wear, which I had borrowed from the university prior to being asked to leave.

My subjects were split up into three groups, each of which was to be shown a video which I had put together in the editing suite. Nowadays, there is dedicated software: I could do it on my laptop at home.

I was planning on testing the power of subliminal messaging, not by flashing up the name of a branded drink or even an exhortation to drink this particular branded drink. It seemed to me that the success of such an experiment would be hard to quantify: a participant who, after seeing the video, chose that particular branded drink, might have chosen it anyway, regardless of the subliminal message. It seemed much more reasonable to assume that nobody coming into the room that day was planning on jumping out of the window.

More specifically, I was aiming to establish which was the more effective: negative suggestion or positive command. I had, in the editing suite, put together three videos. Superficially, they were all the same, a montage of various everyday images.

My morning cohort, Group A, included Mrs Falls. She'd had to bring along her daughter, who was seven years old at the time. The little girl sat on the floor at the back of the room with a drawing pad and some felt-tip pens and a packet of sweets to keep her quiet. "Don't draw on the floor, Bonnie," said Mrs Falls to the little girl, who had not yet uncapped a pen. The little girl looked at the floor, whose vinyl tiles were about the same size and shape as the sheets of paper in her drawing pad, and she took the lid off a pen. I seated my participants so that they were facing both the television screen and, beyond it, the window, which was open, I said, so that the room would not be stifling. I explained to them that I was studying attention span and memory, and that they were required to watch very closely the video which I was about to show to them, and that afterwards there would be a task and questions. And so they watched very closely a video in which I had planted messages which appeared on the screen for a matter of milliseconds. For Group A, in amongst landscape and cityscape and seashore shots, there were positive commands: "FAIL", in capitals in white on black and in black on white, and "JUMP", superimposed on edges, ledges, open windows. ("Fail" is both a positive command and a negative word. In a 2009 article, "Subliminal advertising really does work, claim scientists", the *Telegraph* reported that subjects who were shown negative, neutral and positive subliminal words were more likely to pick up, subconsciously, on the negative ones, such as "despair", and "murder".) When the video came to an end, I realised that I had forgotten to put on my white laboratory coat. I put it on and then asked the participants to take a buzz-wire test. There was a reasonable success rate on the buzz-wire test, which was a disappointment. Mrs Falls managed it: she had a very steady hand. I then asked a series of questions about the video which the group had been shown, keeping them there for longer than I had planned to, but not a single person showed the slightest interest in the open window. I was not, of course, planning on letting anyone actually jump out of the window, but the urge to do so would nonetheless have been evident. I had argued with the university many times about such subtleties.

In between my first two groups, I ate a sandwich. It was during this break that I realised that I had inadvertently watched the first video alongside Group A: I too had been exposed to the "FAIL" and "JUMP" commands. It felt like having stood in the path of an X-ray, an invisible beam of electromagnetic radiation, without having first put on the lead apron. Or perhaps, I thought, the video would not work on me, if I knew that the subliminal messages were there.

I tidied the room up and noticed that the drawing pad had been left behind. On the front, in untidy handwriting, it said "Bonnie Susan Falls", and inside she had drawn a series of rectangles.

After lunch, I welcomed Group B, to whom I showed the same film, except that their subliminal messages were negative suggestions: "DON'T FAIL", in black and white, and "DON'T JUMP", printed like public notices in front of those open windows and at those cliff edges. I watched it with them, hoping that it might neutralise any effect from the first video, that a positive command and a negative command might cancel each other out. Afterwards, they did the buzz-wire test and answered the questions and again showed not the slightest interest in the window, which I had opened a little wider before they came in.

I had hired the community centre for the whole day, but by the afternoon I was running late. I ought to have hired it for two days, or three, but that would have been more expensive. Also, by the middle of the afternoon, I was out of temper because my experiment was not going as I had hoped. I rushed the control group, who were to watch a version of the video which had no subliminal messages in it. I asked them only a few questions before paying them and sending them home. When I was packing up, I discovered that undoctored version of the video still in my bag, which meant that my "control" group must in fact have seen one of the other videos. Probably, I had accidentally reinserted the version that I had shown to Group A, or perhaps I had neglected to swap the tape at all after the Group B showing. Either way, this meant that I had no control group. But never mind, I thought: the experiment had failed anyway. Slight differences between the groups' buzz-wire tests were statistically insignificant, and not one of my subjects had even approached the open window. One woman,

132

who at one point I thought was about to, was only fetching her purse from her bag, so as to show another woman a photograph of her new granddaughter. "Oh," said the other woman, looking at the baby's picture. "She's going to be a heartbreaker."

I typed up my notes, but I was, to be honest, rather put out.

Then, after the passage of some 20 years, I read in the local newspaper about a man who had jumped or fallen from the roof of a car park, and I recognised his name: Eliot Pierce. I dug out my records of my subjects' names, groupings, test scores, and I found that this man had been in Group C: he had been the youngest member of my control group. I remembered that he had worn glasses, and that the lenses were dirty, smudged: he walked around with a big thumbprint—presumably his own, but possibly somebody else's—between him and the world. I had wondered whether his glasses would have prevented him from seeing the video properly, whether everything would have looked blurry, but I suppose not.

The Eliot Pierce incident was the first indication I'd had that there might have been a delayed effect, a result which could not be seen or measured at the time of the experiment. I got in touch with his mother, thinking that we could enlighten one another. I explained who I was, but Mrs Pierce was very unhelpful. I then googled the names of the other participants, in all three groups, but found no further relevant information, which meant that the car park jump was not statistically significant.

At that time, I was living in a house on Slash Lane, which I had converted into flats. The letting was dealt with by an agent—I did not want tenants knocking on my door complaining about blocked toilets or burst pipes. After the student in the ground-floor flat decided to move out, I acquired a new downstairs tenant, who I saw on occasion, when looking out of my front window. She had been in the house for a little while before I found myself going through her paperwork, looking at her name: Falls, Bonnie. As soon as I made the connection, I started to watch her. I observed her coming home from work at the same time every evening, disappearing into the passageway like Mr Hyde heading to his back door.

I made contact, and through Bonnie have had the opportunity of again meeting Mrs Falls, on whom I can see that my subliminal commands had no effect at all.

This reacquaintance with my old experimentees has also brought to mind my little brother's friend, who proved to be a far more cooperative subject for hypnosis than my brother ever was. What I did not know back then is that some people are simply more suggestible than others: they have a suggestible personality, a "hypnotic susceptibility". Hypnosis works "because the subject *believes* the process is effective" (Brown, *Tricks of the Mind*). On the other hand, you can hypnotise a chicken. I understand, though, that this is rather different: the chicken, sensing a threat, enters into a state of semi-paralysis and plays dead. Having failed to hypnotise my brother, and subsequently the cat, neither of them a willing subject, I had more success with my brother's friend, dabbling with hypnosis, the inducement of trance-like states, and post-hypnotic suggestion. I have not thought of him in all this time and now find myself wondering how he is doing.

I have also, of course, had the chance to get to know Bonnie, who was not really a member of the group but who was there at the back of the room throughout the Group A session, doodling in her little book, drawing shapes like that of the television screen at which she kept looking.

At the age of 30, she is inclined to failure. She is drawn, even in her sleep, to windows and edges, and has been known to jump.

18

O N MONDAY MORNING, Bonnie woke up later than she had intended to—it was after nine o'clock—but when she looked out of the front window, she saw that Sylvia was not yet there with the hire car.

Bonnie got dressed and was about to start packing when she realised that she did not have a suitcase. She emptied the dressing-up costumes out of the suitcase in the lounge and used that. She had left her mobile phone charging overnight, and she now unplugged it and put it into her shoulder bag so that she would not forget to take it.

In the middle of the morning, Sylvia pulled up at the kerb and got out of the car looking unusually flustered.

'I'm sorry I'm late,' said Sylvia. 'I just had a few things to finish off.'

'It's fine,' said Bonnie. 'I'm not ready either.' Most of the clothes that she had been planning on bringing were still hanging damp on the line in the yard. She packed them anyway and carried the costumes suitcase out to the car. Lifting it into the boot, she said, 'Have I forgotten anything?'

'If you have,' said Sylvia, 'I'm sure you'll manage.'

'Is that water?' said Bonnie, spying the plastic containers that Sylvia had got in the boot, underneath her own suitcase.

'Be prepared,' said Sylvia, closing the boot. 'We ought to get going.'

'Oh wait!' said Bonnie. 'I knew I'd forgotten something. I'll just be a minute. Come inside and sit down.' Sylvia went with Bonnie back inside the flat, although she did not sit down or take off her jacket, but stood near the door while Bonnie spent a while digging out wellies and waterproof trousers and a waterproof coat. 'You're quite right,' said Bonnie. 'You never know what's going to happen.' Eventually, she set out to the car with her arms full of things that she would not need. Halfway down the passageway, she heard her phone ringing, her landline, or perhaps it was her neighbour's phone. Either way, it soon stopped, and Bonnie had almost reached the car when half the things she was carrying fell into the gutter. With her hair falling into her face, she picked everything up again and put it in the car. Was that everything now? She returned to the house, saying, 'I think I really have remembered everything now.'

'I've got your bag,' said Sylvia, coming through from the lounge into the kitchen.

'Oh yes,' said Bonnie, 'thank you.' She took her bag from Sylvia, glanced cursorily through its contents, and stepped outside, with Sylvia right behind her. As Bonnie turned to lock the door behind them, the house phone started ringing and Bonnie paused with her key in the lock.

'Leave it,' said Sylvia. 'We're on holiday now.'

'Yes,' said Bonnie, locking the door. 'You're right.' They walked through the passageway to the car. They could still hear the phone ringing, but barely, and, when they got into the car and closed the doors, not at all.

Sylvia drove. She did not hold her hands at ten to two on the steering wheel; she held them both at the top, at noon, or midnight, which looked like a dicey way to steer, and Bonnie wondered if she was safe. She also noticed that Sylvia's hands, which had always looked manicured, now looked somewhat scaly. Sylvia picked at the skin on the backs of her hands as she drove, scratching off loose, transparent flakes, and Bonnie saw that it was only glue, dried glue, as if Sylvia had been doing some craftwork, something like papier mâché.

They drove towards the motorway, and when they were nearly at the junction, Sylvia noted that they were passing the site of what had once been a nightclub called The Sea Around Us. The nightclub was now long gone. 'It always seemed like a strange name for a place in the landlocked Midlands,' she said, 'but of course the sea *is* all around us, wherever we are, especially on a small island.' And here and there it was inching closer. Bonnie had seen the information on the Internet about coastal erosion, the predictions for the next twenty and fifty and one hundred years, the places where the cliffs and dunes and beaches were disappearing at the rate of a metre or two or three or more every year.

At the junction, they crossed over the roundabout, going straight past the sign for the M1, 'The SOUTH', where Bonnie had expected to turn off. 'Is that not our exit?' asked Bonnie, turning her head to look back at the signpost for the south, for London.

'No,' said Sylvia. 'That's not the way we're going.'

They left the roundabout again. 'I always wanted to go down to Margate,' said Bonnie. 'I wanted to go to Dreamland, but it closed down years ago.'

'The amusement park?' said Sylvia. 'Wasn't it reopened recently?'

'I wouldn't have thought so,' said Bonnie. 'It's been closed for ten years.'

'I believe it's been refurbished though, and reopened as a "Re-imagined Dreamland".'

'I'd like to go there one day,' said Bonnie. And she thought of going to Butlin's too, although she could hardly believe it still existed beyond the pre-war world of that picture postcard, as if trying to go there would be like trying to get to the Land of Oz.

They got onto a different stretch of road, an A road that turned into a motorway, and Bonnie decided to look these destinations up on her phone, to see if they really did exist and if she could go there. She opened her bag and searched through it. Eventually, she looked up again and said, 'I can't find my phone,' and at the same moment she saw a sign at the side of the road showing the silhouette of an old-fashioned telephone receiver, like the one by her bed, and like the one on a toy phone that she used to have, a phone on wheels, a phone with a face. The silhouette had no cord though, as if the line had been cut through by an intruder. Underneath the disembodied receiver, it said 'SOS'. Half a mile on, she saw another one: 'SOS'. And then another one.

Bonnie felt terribly excited, as if she were Scott of the Antarctic setting out on an expedition, as they drove southwest on the M5—south, with the force of gravity pulling them down, *and underneath*, thought Bonnie, *is everything we don't know and are afraid of knowing*; and west, *go west, young man*, which meant to explore, to seek out new opportunities, but wasn't it also a euphemism for death? 'The South West', said the blue signs, 'The SOUTH WEST', and Bonnie felt like a character in an Alan Sillitoe story she had read, who 'felt like one of those sailors in the olden days who, about to set off west, wasn't sure he would ever get back again'.

The motorway carved through the countryside, and Bonnie saw a lorry full of lambs, and another lorry with 'EAT BRITISH CHICKEN' printed on the back, and another with 'EAT MORE CHIPS' printed on the side, as she and Sylvia sped past. She saw the turn-off for Weston-super-Mare and a brown sign for the Grand Pier. They drove on.

They stopped for a late lunch at Sedgemoor services. Out of the air-conditioned car, they could feel the mid-July heat. 'You wouldn't know we were in England,' said Bonnie. 'We could be abroad.'

They bought sandwiches and giant cups of tea and sat down. Bonnie rummaged around in her shoulder bag. 'I still can't find my phone,' she said.

'Maybe you left it at home,' said Sylvia.

'I remember putting it in my bag,' said Bonnie. 'I'm sure I did . . .'

'The mind can play tricks,' said Sylvia.

They ate their sandwiches, though Bonnie left her crusts.

'You should eat your crusts,' said Sylvia. 'They're good for you.'

'I'm going to give them to the birds,' said Bonnie.

Outside, while she smoked a cigarette, she scattered the crusts for the car-park pigeons, and then Bonnie and Sylvia returned to the car and the M5. Bonnie, in the passenger seat, was rooting around again in the bag on her lap. 'What on earth have I done with my phone?' she muttered.

'Forget about your phone,' said Sylvia. 'We're on holiday.'

'I'll need to phone my mum when we arrive,' said Bonnie, 'to let her know I'm safe.'

'I would lend you my phone,' said Sylvia, 'if I had one. They're bound to have a phone in the pub though. I'm sure you'll be able to use that.'

Sylvia put on one of her CDs, her film music, and Bonnie watched the landscape scrolling by, within the frame of the passenger-seat window.

They were less than an hour from Seaton when they turned off the motorway and onto A roads that wound through the villages. At one junction, they took a wrong turn—someone had tampered with the signpost, turning the arm to point the wrong way, like a comic-book jape. They got onto a B road, which would take them all the way down to the sea. Poppies growing in the verge made Bonnie think of Dorothy en route to the Emerald City, watched by the Wicked Witch of the West through her crystal ball, Dorothy fast asleep in a field of poppies, in which she might sleep forever. The poppies looked as if they were made of red tissue paper or crepe paper.

It was all downhill as they neared the sea, and the car picked up speed. They crossed the River Axe and entered Seaton on the Harbour Road.

'I'm really looking forward to this,' said Sylvia, reaching over to the passenger seat and gripping Bonnie's forearm, and her skinny, sharp-nailed fingers made Bonnie think of those stories of seagulls trying to fly off with cats and small dogs. Then Sylvia returned her hand to its worrying position on the steering wheel, braking gently as they approached the corner. 'Here we are,' she said, although their view was obscured by a derelict block of flats, and then they turned the final bend, and Bonnie saw the sea.

Sylvia slowed, and stopped, and backed into a tight space between two parked cars, with the pounding sea on one side and the Hook and Parrot on the other.

'So here it is,' said Sylvia. 'This is where your story takes place.'

'It's a long time since I've been here,' said Bonnie, peering through the passenger window.

'Come on,' said Sylvia, reaching across and unbuckling Bonnie's seat belt. Sylvia climbed out from behind the steering wheel and went around to the passenger side to open Bonnie's door, shepherding her out of the car.

Bonnie noticed the pay and display sign that was screwed to the wall. Reading it, she said to Sylvia, 'You can't park here for more than four hours.'

'Don't worry about that,' said Sylvia. 'I'll move it later.'

Bonnie went round to the boot to get their suitcases out.

'Leave the suitcases for now,' said Sylvia. 'We can do that later.'

Bonnie looked at the Hook and Parrot's facade. 'It's not how I remember it,' she said. She turned to face the ancient sea, and took a deep breath of sea air.

'We'll go for a little walk first,' said Sylvia, 'and then we'll go inside.'

They walked along the concrete esplanade, passing a woman whose face was made up like an actor's, like a chorus girl's; her make-up was heavy enough to show up under stage lights.

'Look,' said Sylvia, pointing to the ground, 'Here's one of the signs you put into your story.' The letters painted onto the concrete said 'NO CYCLING'. They walked on, and Sylvia pointed out the other signs that said 'Dogs not allowed' and, next to a picture of a seagull, 'PLEASE DON'T FEED ME'.

When they reached the storm gates in between the esplanade and the beach, Bonnie said, 'Let's go back now.'

141

'We'll go to the pub and have something to eat,' said Sylvia. 'Then we'll go up to our rooms, and maybe actually being there will help you find the ending to your story.'

The front of the Hook and Parrot was white, or almost white, white with a hint of purple, or white with an old layer of purple underneath, almost showing through. Or perhaps it was just the light; perhaps it was just white.

It was the strangest thing, to walk inside the Hook. It was like walking into a story, although, at the same time, it wasn't. Bonnie looked around at the interior, which was nothing like in her story. She had never actually been inside the Hook; she had only used the name and apart from that had made it up entirely.

'I'll get us some drinks and menus,' said Sylvia, 'while you go and sit down.'

'A lemonade for me, please,' said Bonnie.

'Diet?' said Sylvia.

'All right,' said Bonnie. 'Thanks.'

Bonnie went over to a window seat, facing the bar and a display of peanuts. She fancied some peanuts. Just next to the bar, there was a row of gumball machines. She liked gumball machines; putting a coin into a gumball machine was like playing a slot machine but winning every time.

There was hardly anyone else in the pub, only a trio of men at the bar, whose conversation she could hear. Two of the men, who had each bought a round, while the third man had not, were joking about this other man having short arms. 'My arms *are* short,' said the man. 'And so are my dad's, and so were *his* dad's. I swear to you,' he said, 'I am evidence of a Victorian breeding programme designed to breed children with short arms so that they couldn't touch their privates at night. You know how they were always tucked very tight into their beds so they wouldn't play with themselves? Well, in this case, the Victorians were, instead, engineering shorter arms to put a stop to the fiddling.' The other men laughed, and the man with the short arms shook his head. 'Seriously,' he said, 'look at me,' and he reached out with his short arm for his pint.

'Here we are,' said Sylvia, coming over to the window seat with two drinks and a menu. Both the drinks looked the same, and Bonnie put her hand out for one. 'Not that one,' said Sylvia. 'It's got vodka in it,' she added, pushing the other glass towards Bonnie, who could not tell the difference by looking. 'This one's yours.' Bonnie took her diet lemonade, which was fizzing fast, like speeded-up film.

They sipped their drinks and looked at the menu. 'I think I'll have the Lyme Bay Crab Salad,' said Sylvia. Bonnie had seen crabs being caught by the holidaymakers in Lyme Regis: surprisingly tiny crabs, babies, put into buckets of sun-warming water lined up on the harbour wall. She had wanted to tip them back into the sea. She worried about them being put into car boots and forgotten about until they started to smell of death.

'I'll have the Cheesy Chips,' said Bonnie.

'They've got desserts as well, if you want one,' said Sylvia. 'Various things with custard.'

'I don't like custard,' said Bonnie. She had not been able to eat it since she ate a bowl of custard in the garden when she was little, and swallowed what felt like glass. 'Grass?' said her mother, when Bonnie ran into the kitchen to tell her. 'Glass,' said Bonnie. 'It won't have been glass,' said her mother. 'Perhaps it was an insect. It won't hurt you.' And as

Bonnie got older, she too thought: *It can't have been glass*, even though such things did happen, such things did get into food; but still, she thought, it was probably a blade of grass, which can cut like paper, or else an insect with a sting. She could still not eat a bowl of custard though. She was generally wary of food that she had not prepared herself, even though she was no cook.

'Shall I go and order?' asked Bonnie, unzipping her purse, which was stuffed with old receipts and all sorts of things that she pulled out, searching for paper money.

Sylvia picked something out of all the litter. 'What's this?' she asked.

Bonnie looked at the little origami figure that Sylvia was holding. 'I found it in my flat,' she said, 'in the desk drawer. I think it's some sort of bird, a flightless bird, like a chicken or a dodo.'

'It's a chicken,' said Sylvia. 'My grandmother used to make these. She showed me how to do it when I was little. I could probably do it now. You don't forget these things once they're in your head.' Bonnie gave her the silver paper from inside her cigarette packet, and watched as Sylvia folded it corner to corner, folded again, turned it and lifted a flap and refolded, and already Bonnie was quite lost and would never have been able to retrace the steps. She had never even known how to make a paper hat or a boat. All of a sudden, there it was, standing on the table in front of her: a silver-paper chicken, and Bonnie thought of *Blade Runner*, and the cop saying, *It's too bad she won't live. But then again, who does?*, like the chaplain in *The Outsider* who said that everyone was condemned to death: *if you don't die soon, you'll die one day.*

144

'Chickens aren't really flightless, you know,' said Sylvia, 'unless they've had their wings clipped. They can fly, they just tend not to; they don't really need to, unless they feel they're in danger.'

Bonnie put the litter back into her purse, leaving the paper chickens standing on the table like two sentry guards. She started to get to her feet. 'If I go and order,' she said, 'I can ask about the room, and the phone.'

'I'll go,' said Sylvia, standing up. 'I'm nearer than you, and I have the booking reference.'

While Sylvia went to the bar, Bonnie sat and looked out of the window, thinking about Lyme Regis, which was mentioned in the shipping forecast, which Bonnie heard in the dead of night: Selsey Bill to Lyme Regis, and Lyme Regis to Land's End; fair, moderate, occasionally very poor, and then 'God Save the Queen'.

She sat with the big oblong windows in between her and the climbing sea, and waited.

19

BONNIE WOKE FEELING heavy, as if she had fallen asleep on the beach in the sun, except that she was in a bedroom, tucked up in bed, underneath a yellow blanket. Her arm was flung back, bent beneath her head, and she had to move it with her other hand so as to get the blood back into it. The dead weight was unsettling—*like a ten-pound leg of lamb lying on the pillow*, she thought.

It was dusk, or dawn. She could see the sky through a curtainless window. She was in her room above the Hook, of course. She was in Susan's room. How funny, she thought, that the window really did have no curtains.

The journey must have been more tiring than she had realised. She remembered being downstairs in the bar with Sylvia. Sylvia had been talking about chickens and how they could be hypnotised. 'I put a finger just in front of the chicken's beak,' she had said, 'not quite touching,' and she had put her finger close to the end of Bonnie's nose as if to demonstrate, 'and then I draw my finger away a little,' she said, as she did so, 'and then I bring it back . . . And I do this until my chicken is hypnotised.'

Bonnie had no recollection of coming to bed. She did not even remember getting undressed, but she must have done so because she was wearing the nightie from her suitcase, which Sylvia must have brought in. Bonnie knew for certain that she had only been drinking diet lemonade. Or perhaps her drinks had got mixed up with Sylvia's after all. Wasn't it vodka, she thought, that you could not taste?

How strange, she considered, looking around, that she had got the room so right, or nearly right. Or perhaps it was not so strange, for it was only a room with a bed in it, and a wardrobe, and a desk with writing paper and a pen on it; you would find these things in any hotel room. As in her story, the wallpaper was floral, but only one of these walls was papered, while the other three were painted white, or off-white: it was a trick, she thought, to make the room look bigger than it really was. The wallpaper's almost psychedelic design was not exactly what she had pictured, and the patterned carpet was busier than she had imagined. There were other differences too: there was a picture hanging on the partition wall opposite the window, just as there was in her Seatown story, and it was even a Cézanne, and one of the apple paintings as well, but it was not the right one, and it was a rather poor quality print in an ill-fitting frame. And there were three doors in the walls, like one of those riddles in which you have to make the right choice because one of the doors has something really terrible behind it.

One of the doors was in the corner diagonally across from the bed, and the other two were facing that one. She did not know which of them led to the outside world, and which just led into a cupboard.

Apart from these differences, though, it was astonishing the extent to which this room was like Susan's, which had only ever existed in Bonnie's mind, or so she had thought. It made her wonder if she had in fact been in this room before and had just forgotten, or half-forgotten.

The lack of curtains was rather strange, but it did not bother her too much. If the room was in the attic, it was not like anyone walking by could see in.

She wanted to sit up—she could see her cigarettes on the windowsill—but her limbs were sluggish. As she struggled up from the mattress, there was a knock at the door in the furthest corner of the room, and no pause before it opened and there was Sylvia, coming in with a breakfast tray.

'Are you feeling any better?' asked Sylvia.

'Have I been ill?' asked Bonnie. 'Am I ill?'

'You weren't too good last night,' said Sylvia, propping her up with pillows and setting the tray down on Bonnie's lap: a glass of orange juice, a small plate of scrambled eggs, and a cup of tea. 'You'll want to stay in bed today. You'll find your legs are weak, too weak to walk on just yet.'

Sylvia sat down next to Bonnie, and Bonnie ate. Her appetite was fine. 'I don't remember coming upstairs last night,' she said.

'No,' said Sylvia. 'But you seem much better now.'

'It's so strange being in this room,' said Bonnie. 'It's a lot like the room in my story, weirdly so in some ways, although in other ways it's different.'

'In what ways is it different?' asked Sylvia, frowning around at the room.

'Well, there's a clock on that wall,' said Bonnie, 'which isn't there in my story.' The clock, which had a big, round, white face, was on the same wall as the Cézanne.

'You didn't mention it in your story,' said Sylvia. 'That is true.'

'And the Cézanne isn't the right one,' said Bonnie.

'Isn't it?' said Sylvia.

'And the room's the wrong shape,' said Bonnie.

'Well I don't see what anyone could do about that,' said Sylvia.

'It's very strange though,' said Bonnie, 'that the room should be so similar, because as far as I know I've never been up here before.'

'Well you obviously *have*,' said Sylvia. 'You've just forgotten. The subconscious is a powerful thing.'

When Bonnie finished her scrambled eggs, she picked up her teacup. The saucer and her empty plate, side by side like a pair of staring eyes, shared a design of black and white concentric circles. She turned to look again at the pack of cigarettes on the windowsill. 'Would you mind passing me my cigarettes?' she asked.

'You must not smoke,' said Sylvia. 'Let's leave them there for now. Your room, by the way, is at the back of the building; I couldn't get you a sea view, I'm afraid. But you'll be able to hear the seagulls.' And Bonnie could.

'Do you think I could have some curtains?' asked Bonnie.

'We'll see,' said Sylvia, taking the tray from Bonnie's lap and standing up.

'Could you ask the landlady?'

Sylvia smiled. 'You get some rest now,' she said, moving the pillows that were propping Bonnie up. 'You'll be feeling sleepy.' She helped Bonnie to lie down again, and pulled the yellow blanket over her, up to her neck. 'You close your eyes and have a little nap.'

Sylvia stroked Bonnie's hair, slowly, the rhythm of it closing Bonnie's eyes.

When Bonnie woke again, she saw, in the weak daylight, on the carpet by the door, the edge of a piece of paper, like a note that had been pushed through the gap at the bottom of the door.

She made an effort to sit up, but one leg was lying lifeless beneath the other and she had to lift it with both hands, holding it under the thigh. She hung the numb limb over the side of her bed and sat waiting for it to fizz back to life.

After a while, she tried putting her weight on her feet, looking down at the carpet, whose geometric design was reminiscent of an optical illusion. When she stood up, she felt fine, not especially ill nor very dizzy, although as she stepped forward, moving towards the door, she felt like one of those newborn foals standing, trying to walk, for the very first time. She bent down carefully and picked the piece of paper up, looked at one side and then the other, but it was blank—although there was, when she turned the paper towards the light and inspected it closely, the faintest suggestion of words there, the shadow of something that had been photocopied almost to oblivion. She put her hand on the door handle. She half-felt that if she opened it and looked outside she would find nothing but desert, and that if she walked through the doorway she would never get back inside again. She opened the door, and it felt unexpectedly light in her hand. It was not solid wood; it was a cheap hardboard door, but newly painted. Outside, there was an empty landing, and the top of a flight of stairs, the sight of which made her head swim. She felt blurry. She had in mind to go and look for Sylvia, but her legs felt both weak and heavy and she wanted to go back to bed. 'Sylvia?' she called. 'Sylvia?' She heard a noise and a door further along the landing opened.

'Bonnie!' said Sylvia. 'You're out of bed!'

Sylvia came to the door of Bonnie's room and took her by the elbow, and Bonnie said, 'Did you put this under my door?'

'Put what under your door?' asked Sylvia.

'It's some kind of note, I think,' said Bonnie. She looked again at the piece of paper in her hand, and almost thought that she might be able to make out a message after all, but even as she looked, that hint of words dissolved, as a mirage dissolves.

Bonnie left the piece of paper on the desk near the door, and Sylvia walked her back over to her bed.

'I need to go to the toilet,' said Bonnie.

'There's a toilet just there,' said Sylvia, indicating one of the doors that Bonnie had taken for a cupboard.

'I wasn't expecting an en suite,' said Bonnie.

'You have everything you need right here,' said Sylvia. 'You don't have to leave your room for anything. I'll look after you.' Sylvia held out her arm, and Bonnie, in her nightie, took it. She crossed the room, walking the length of that complicated carpet, with her arm linked through Sylvia's, as if this were her wedding day, as if Sylvia were giving her away.

'Here we are,' said Sylvia, when they reached the door.

Bonnie went in to use the toilet. There was no window in there so she switched on the light, and shut the door for privacy. 'There's even a shower in here,' she said to Sylvia, through the closed door. 'I could do with a shower, a bit later maybe. What happened last night?' she asked. 'It's like one minute we were sitting downstairs and the next minute I was waking up here.' She pressed the flush but nothing happened. She tried again. 'The flush isn't working,' she said, but Sylvia did not answer. Bonnie turned on the tap but no water came out. 'I think there's a problem with the water,' she said. 'We ought to let the landlady know.'

Bonnie opened the door and looked out, but Sylvia was not there. Bonnie made her way back across the room to her bed. She sat down. A tapping sound at the window made her turn her head: a seagull had perched on the sill outside and was rapping on the glass with its beak. The gull appeared to be looking at her, but Bonnie could not tell whether it could really see her or only its own reflection. It flew away.

Bonnie tried to remember whether she had phoned her mother after arriving in Seaton. Sylvia had gone to the bar to order food, and had come back to say that she had asked about using the phone, and that it would be fine to do so but that the line was out of order and was at that moment being fixed, and that she would be welcome to use it as soon as it was mended. Bonnie had not, as far as she could remember, made her call.

Sylvia came into the room with a tray, on which was a plate of toast and a cup of tea.

'I want to phone my mum,' said Bonnie.

'Yes,' said Sylvia, setting the tray down on Bonnie's lap. 'But we haven't got a phone, have we? And we're out of range here anyway.'

'But the pub's got a phone. I can use that.'

'Yes,' said Sylvia. 'I'll ask if it's been fixed yet, and then if you're strong enough I'll take you downstairs so that you can phone your mother and tell her that you're safe.'

Bonnie ate her buttered toast, and Sylvia said, 'It's not true, you know, that we swallow eight spiders a year in our sleep. It's a complete fabrication, but the statistic is decades old and continues to circulate on the Internet. It goes to show how keen we are to believe what we see.'

'I didn't really think it was true,' said Bonnie.

'It's probably more like one or two,' said Sylvia. 'By the way, when Joe asked Susan why he would be slipping notes under her door and sticking them onto her window, why did you star-out the word "fucking"?'

'I couldn't write that,' said Bonnie. 'My mum might read it.'

'I don't really see why you need the swearing at all,' said Sylvia. 'And you shouldn't start a sentence with "and" or "but". It's bad form.'

Bonnie nodded and drank her tea. As she put her cup down again, she shivered.

'Are you cold?' asked Sylvia. 'You didn't bring a jumper with you, but I've got one you can wear.' And she produced from somewhere, like a magic trick, or perhaps just out of a bedside drawer, a thin, blue jumper. She helped Bonnie to pull it on. 'There,' she said. She took the tray away, glancing back at Bonnie when she reached the door. Smiling, she left the room.

Bonnie looked at the clock on the wall and realised that the hands were not moving. It occurred to her that she had no idea what time of day it was. The meal—the toast and tea—could have been breakfast or supper. She wondered where her watch was: it was not on her wrist. She could not see her shoulder bag anywhere, but she knew that her mobile phone was not in it anyway. Not knowing what time it was, she could not even be sure what day it was. She would have to ask Sylvia.

She lay in bed, waiting to see whether it was going to get lighter or darker.

Eventually, with the window still framing a wide, blue sky, she fell asleep. The lack of curtains only troubled her when she woke in the night and saw the cold window with all that darkness outside, that big black rectangle in the middle of the long wall.

In her dream, Bonnie had jumped into a swimming pool. She was going down and down, feet first; the pool was impossibly

154

deep, but it had no water in it. She felt her feet touch the white-tiled bottom, and remembered nothing after that.

Bonnie opened her eyes and lay looking at the uncurtained window, in the middle of which she could see a small, white square. She sat up, peering at it, trying to see what it was. It was clear that it was not a reflection of the Cézanne, the wrong apples, next to which a reflection of the broken clock would have hung like a moon.

There was no lamp on the bedside table, so she climbed out of bed and crossed the room in the dark. She reached out and touched the white square, a sheet of paper, which was stuck to the inside of the glass. On the page, she thought she could see, despite the darkness, the word 'JUMP'. She unstuck the paper from the window, took it over to the desk and switched on the Anglepoise lamp, which spilt a pool of yellow light across the desktop. With the light on, she felt exposed to the outside world, which she could not see; if she looked at the window, she saw only her own reflection, as if she were standing in front of a one-way mirror in an investigation room.

Looking at the paper in the light, she found that there was nothing written on it after all, and even when she switched the lamp off again and looked at the page in darkness as before, she could see nothing there.

She went to the door of her room, but when she tried to open it she found it resistant, as if she were pulling when she ought to be pushing. Eventually, she realised that it was locked. Bonnie knocked on her door, from the inside. 'Sylvia?' she called. 'Sylvia?' But no one answered.

She turned away from the door and stood in the middle of the room, listening for sounds of breathing, hearing nothing.

She scrunched up the piece of paper, dropped it into the wastepaper basket and went back to bed. She thought she might lie awake until it got light, but she must have fallen straight back to sleep because suddenly she was waking again. On the edge of sleep, she heard music, a song she knew—*Last night as I lay on my pillow*—the lines looping through her head—*Last night as I lay on my bed*—like the language she was supposed to be learning—*Last night as I lay on my pillow*—or like the lessons learnt by the children in *Brave New World*—*I dreamt that my Bonnie was dead.* What an odd song, she thought as she came awake, to hear in a pub in the depths of the night. Or perhaps it was only the remnant of a dream, because at that moment, the music stopped.

It was still dark. And there, again, in the middle of the window, was a familiar white square. She stared at it, knowing that if she crossed the room and tried to touch the piece of paper that was stuck to the glass, she would find that she could not: her fingers would slip right over it as if it were frozen beneath ice. She crept to the end of her bed, towards the closed window, through which she could hear the sea and the crying of gulls, which sounded like laughter, and she said to them, through the glass, 'Don't you sleep?'

There did seem to be something written on the piece of paper. It was not quite legible, but Bonnie believed that she could almost see the hint of the word that was written there: 'JUMP'.

Her pack of cigarettes was still on the windowsill. It was face up, and the label said 'Smoking kills'. Bonnie extracted a cigarette, reached for the window handle and eased the window open. It was astonishingly dark out there: there were no lit street lamps, or stars visible in the sky; there was no moon. She could barely see the pavement below. In the darkness, she could hear very clearly the pull of the tide. But where was her lighter? It was not in the packet with the cigarettes, nor loose on the windowsill. Perhaps it was in her shoulder bag, which she did not have. She pulled the window to again and put the unsmoked cigarette back inside the packet. She went back to her bed and her pillow.

She dreamt about nothing.

'My door was locked,' said Bonnie to Sylvia, who was coming into the room with a bowl of ice cream, like Bonnie's mother when Bonnie had her tonsils removed.

'Sorry, Bonnie,' said Sylvia, shutting the door behind her and coming over to the bed. 'I decided to lock your door because you've not been well, sometimes hardly able to get out of bed, and if you couldn't get to the door to lock it from the inside, I had to lock it from the outside, to keep you safe. That makes sense, doesn't it?'

'And I still don't know where my bag is,' said Bonnie.

'Have you not got it?' asked Sylvia. 'I'm sure it will turn up before we leave.'

'I saw another note,' said Bonnie.

'Another note?' said Sylvia.

'Yes,' said Bonnie. 'Like the one I found under the door yesterday, except that this one was on the window.'

Sylvia frowned. She put her hand to Bonnie's forehead. 'You ought to rest,' she said. 'You've not been well.'

'I would like to get some fresh air though,' said Bonnie. 'I'd really like to go down to the seafront.'

'Soon,' said Sylvia, 'perhaps.'

Bonnie was feeling rather weak in the legs anyway. She ate her vanilla ice cream, and Sylvia said, 'Where is this note?'

'I'm sure I left the first note on the desk,' said Bonnie. 'But it's gone now. I threw the second note in the wastepaper basket.'

Sylvia went over to the wastepaper basket. 'The basket is empty,' she said.

'Yes,' said Bonnie. 'And there was a third one as well, stuck to the outside of the window,' but they could both see, even as she was saying it, that there was nothing there now.

'I think you've been dreaming,' said Sylvia. 'Or hallucinating.'

Sylvia herself did not look entirely well, thought Bonnie. She looked rather wide-eyed. Her complexion was shiny and her hair was quite wild. She still had on what might have been the same blue suit, and it looked a little dishevelled. Perhaps this sea air was not doing either of them any good.

'You're getting mixed up with what happens in your Seatown story,' said Sylvia. 'It's not surprising, of course. Here you are, in Susan's room, in Susan's bed, almost in Susan's skin. Now you can find your ending. You just have to think: what is she going to do?'

'I don't know,' said Bonnie.

'Well, as long as you're in the right frame of mind, in your character's mindset, it will come. You're Susan—what happens next?'

Bonnie finished her ice cream and Sylvia took the bowl away, and Bonnie heard her lock the door.

Bonnie woke suddenly, from a dream in which she had dived into water, into the sea, and was looking around on the seabed for something that she had lost. She had been underwater for a very long time, and throughout she had been holding her breath.

She seemed to remember from reading Freud that a dream of diving into water was a 'crossing a threshold' symbol relating to the process of waking. It seemed topsy-turvy, because the sea was supposed to be the realm of dreams. In dreams, though, there was all this reversal.

And she had, just before waking, found what she had been looking for, which was a key, a car key. She had lifted it from where it was lying half-buried in the sand, like a gift from the sea.

She could feel something tickling her cheek, and she scratched and rubbed at her face.

She was on the edge of the mattress. She rolled back into the middle of the bed and looked at the window, the night sky. There was no moon—no circle, and no square either. She got out of bed and turned on the desk lamp. Squinting away from the light, she looked down at the headache-inducing carpet, which she could see now had not been properly laid, only cut to size; she could see the loose threads from the rough edges against the skirting boards.

Facing the window, she found that her reflection was missing, as if somehow she did not exist, but then she saw that the window was wide open; it must have been left ajar and caught by the wind. She shivered in the night air and thought that it was lucky that the glass in the flung-open window had not smashed. The draught coming in, blowing the split ends of her hair against her face, must have been what woke her up.

She could smell something damp in the room, something mouldering, a swampy smell.

And then she saw the word.

20

THERE WAS A word on the window. It looked etched into the glass itself, scratched with something sharp, like the point of a compass, and she remembered a boy at school using the point of a compass to scratch a message into his own arm. She did not remember what it was that he scored into his flesh, but it was something short, and perhaps left unfinished.

She went to the window and ran the tip of her forefinger along the length of the word: 'JUMP'. The surface of the glass was smooth, though; she could see but not feel the engraving. It seemed to be *inside* the glass, like the warning that appeared like an advertisement within the window of an electric tram in an M. R. James story. What were the words that appeared there? It was, she thought, some lines from 'The Rime of the Ancient Mariner', about someone who, having glanced over his shoulder, *walks on,*

> *And turns no more his head;*
> *Because he knows a frightful fiend*
> *Doth close behind him tread.*

Or perhaps that appeared somewhere else in the story. She had a feeling that what was seen within the window of the tram was a message with a more specific hint of what was coming, but she could not quite remember what it was.

She wanted to touch the outside of the window to see if the writing had somehow been scratched on backwards from the outside. She thought that this message was not quite so far beyond her reach as the previous one had been.

She took her pack of cigarettes from the windowsill. The lighter was inside the packet, where it belonged. She lit up a cigarette and leaned out of the window to puff out the smoke. She could hear the harsh utterances of the gulls, and the sound of the sea toying with the pebbles at its edge, and she flicked her ash to the ground. In a vacuum, or on the moon, she would fall at the same speed as that ash, at the same speed as a feather. She was not in a vacuum though; she was not on the moon.

Light was leaking into the sky. The tide would be coming in.

It seemed to her that it mattered greatly whether the word had somehow appeared *within* the glass or whether it had been scratched into the glass from the far side. She reached around, trying to touch the outside of the window, but her arm was too short. She got herself up onto the windowsill and tried again, straining towards that hard-to-reach spot behind the word. Her fingertips, with their bitten nails, edged closer. 'Come on,' she murmured, 'come on,' and she leaned out just a little further.

Her cigarette landed last, and softly.

Keep passing the open windows.
– John Irving, *The Hotel New Hampshire*

21

S HE KNEW THAT was how it had to end. As soon as she had seen that word, which really did seem to be scratched into the pane of glass in the unfastened window, Bonnie had known suddenly and clearly what she had to do. Still in that place between sleeping and fully waking, she had turned away from the wide-open window and written the last part of her story out in longhand in the lamplight, without even sitting down at the desk, only leaning over the desktop to scribble onto the paper, giving herself a backache. She felt strongly, unequivocally, that it was the only possible conclusion, although she would want to check that reference to 'Casting the Runes', that Coleridge quotation.

So, she thought, as she put down her pen, her story was finished, although she still did not know why the messages had appeared in Susan's room, or who had put them there. It was the landlady, she supposed; she had wanted to see what would happen. People did some very odd things. Or at least the landlady was responsible for the first message. Beyond that, perhaps it had just been Susan's imagination. Or perhaps it was all in her imagination; perhaps she had dreamt the whole thing. Perhaps, at the end, she was sleepwalking.

Straightening up, Bonnie became aware that the door to her room was standing slightly open, creaking in the breeze. She stepped away from the desk and went towards the door. She looked outside, peering up and down the dark landing. 'Sylvia?' she said, but there was no reply. She stepped onto the landing.

The door adjacent to hers was ajar, and Bonnie hesitated only briefly before entering this neighbouring room. Even in the dim light of dawn, Bonnie could see that Sylvia was not in there, although she switched the light on anyway. Not only was Sylvia not in her bed but there was no bed; there was no furniture at all except for a table standing against the wall. Everything was bare: the walls and the gappy floorboards and the lightbulb hanging from the ceiling. Only Bonnie's room had been given a fresh coat of paint, and decorated with a few rolls of end-of-line floral wallpaper and cut-to-size patterned carpet and a Cézanne that might have been printed off the Internet, the bed dressed with Susan's yellow blanket.

The table, which was standing against the partition wall, was the one with folding legs from the under-stairs cupboard, and on it stood an open laptop. On the screen, Bonnie could see what she realised was her own room, as if the screen were a one-way window; she could see the bed in which she had just been sleeping, and the wide-open window from which Susan had fallen. A wire snaked out of the side of the laptop and up the wall, up to a finger-sized hole that had been drilled through the brickwork. It reminded her of artworks that she had seen that invited people to look through peep-holes. The wire disappeared into the hole, and would come out, she guessed, on the far side, just where the clock that did not tell the time had been hung on the wall. If she were to stand in her own room in front of the clock, her face would appear on the screen of the laptop in Sylvia's room.

Next to the laptop was a notepad whose handwritten entries said things such as '9.46pm awake'. Beside the notepad were a few old typewritten pages, stapled together in one corner. The pages included, saw Bonnie, browsing through, a list of names, split into three groups, in the first of which Bonnie saw her mother's name, and, inserted in pencil, a reference to herself: 'Bonnie Falls, 7 years old'. Her skin prickled as if chilled by a draught. There was also a more recent, word-processed document—something like a report, with citations. Flicking through the loose pages, she saw 'Bonnie has failed', 'free will is an illusion', 'FAIL' and 'JUMP', and something about chickens. Towards the back, she found what seemed to be a summary or critique of the dissertation that she had never written, and a newspaper clipping about Eliot Pierce and his plunge from the top of the three-storey car park in town. He had landed badly and had been in a coma, but he was all right, he was going to be all right, as far as Bonnie knew. On the last page, like a final thought, was a single handwritten paragraph: 'Eliot Pierce was 18, only just on the brink of adulthood, and Bonnie Falls was still an infant. Might young people be more susceptible to subliminal messages than older people are? They are certainly more suggestible. A number of reports document the suggestibility of children, especially very young children, whose memories are malleable, their narratives changeable, conforming to the adults' suggestions. It should be quite easy to test whether these very young children are also more susceptible to subliminal messages.'

There was a used coffee cup on the table, and an Anglepoise lamp, and an empty CD case with a handwritten label on the front saying 'BONNIE SEASIDE'.

Underneath the table, Bonnie found her shoulder bag, inside which she located her lighter; and in Sylvia's bag, Bonnie discovered her missing phone, along with the car keys, and a paper bag with something hard and round inside it, like a cartoon bomb, wrapped in layers of tissue paper and bubble wrap. Beneath these layers, she found a teapot, with 'Seatown' written on the side.

She could not see her suitcase. And where was Sylvia? She was not in the little bathroom that adjoined this would-be bedroom. Bonnie opened the other door next to the bathroom, which was not a cupboard but a kitchenette, with a lukewarm kettle on the side, and those plastic water containers that Sylvia had brought along, and a toaster, and a half-empty jar of instant coffee and a spoon, and a little stack of clean crockery and Tupperware tubs on a tray, and a window that had a view of the sea and was within sight of the Hook and Parrot, which was a few hundred metres down the road.

Bonnie returned to her own room. There was light in the sky now. She looked in the wardrobe and under the bed, where she found her suitcase, and when she opened it up she found it full of her damp and mouldering clothes. The clothes that she had travelled down in were in there too and had become equally damp, but she put them on. She felt like something that had just crawled out of the sea.

There was still some life in her phone, and there was a signal. She had lots of missed calls, from home, from her mother, who Bonnie called now. She hoped that she would not hear the answerphone—'Please, please, please,' she said to the phone—and then she heard her mother's voice, saying, 'Bonnie? Bonnie? Is that you? Where are you?'

'I'm still at the seaside,' said Bonnie, 'but I'm coming home.'

'Oh thank God,' said her mother. 'Are you with Sylvia?'

'I don't know where she is,' said Bonnie.

'Your Sylvia is Dr Slythe, did you know that?'

'I didn't know,' said Bonnie.

'I told you all about her, years ago, about that experiment she conducted at the community centre, and what Eliot Pierce's mother told me Dr Slythe was really doing.'

Bonnie did not remember her mother mentioning it. Or perhaps it did ring a bell, being told about this bogus doctor and her dubious and potentially dangerous experiment; she had all but forgotten about it.

'Do you think I'd have come on holiday with her,' said Bonnie, 'if I'd realised it was her?'

'I suddenly realised who she was, just when you were leaving. I phoned your flat, but Sylvia answered. I told her I knew who she was, and told her to put you on the phone, not to take you away, but she hung up. I tried your mobile, but I couldn't get you.'

'Sylvia had my mobile,' said Bonnie.

'Is she there?' asked her mother.

'She's here somewhere,' said Bonnie. 'She's been up to her tricks again. I'm not sure where she's gone though.'

'But you're going to come home?'

'Yes.'

'Are you all right?' asked her mother. 'You don't sound all right.'

'I'm a bit cold,' said Bonnie. 'My clothes are damp.'

'Oh Bonnie,' said her mother. 'You'll catch your death.' She sighed. 'I'm not sure you'd have been out of harm's way here either though. That friend of yours from the laboratory—'

'Fiona?' said Bonnie.

'Well, that's not her real name. She was with an animal liberation group. They had a plan to release the animals that were being experimented on. They locked your supervisor in a store room. And someone started a fire in the outbuildings, which spread.'

Bonnie thought about the animals, what might have been done to them, how they might be damaged; she wondered how they would fare now, in the outside world.

'So you're coming home?' asked her mother.

'Yes,' said Bonnie. 'I'm coming now.'

'You're not going to drive, are you?'

Bonnie half-heard her father saying something in the background. She could just picture him insisting, *You'll crash!*

'I'll be fine,' said Bonnie.

It was only after hanging up that she realized she had not asked her mother if the animals had in fact been freed, if the plan had gone as intended.

She took her suitcase to the door, put the ending to her story in her bag and picked her cigarettes up off the windowsill. She inspected that word that had appeared in or on the glass. Putting her finger to it, she could feel that nothing had been scratched in from this side of the window. She was reaching out of the open window for the handle when she noticed that what was written there was not 'JUMP' but 'JUMI', and she wondered what that might mean, and then it occurred to her that it was more

170

likely to be that someone had not quite finished scratching the intended word into the glass, from the far side.

A little bit of blue down below drew her eye, and when she looked she saw Sylvia, lying on the slabs.

Out on the landing again, Bonnie gripped the banister, which was not made of wood but cold metal. She felt light-headed, weak-limbed. She had brought the yellow blanket with her, as if it were her comforter.

She descended the stairs. Below the carpeted landing, the concrete staircase was bare, and it did not spiral down but turned corner after corner, going down to a ground floor that was not white-and-red tiled, and there were no boxes of bar snacks at the bottom, and there was no bar. The building looked as if it had not been inhabited for months, or longer. It looked as if it had been gutted for redevelopment, or else it had been earmarked for demolition.

There was an emergency exit sign above a door that had a metal bar across it, the sort that you had to push down, the sort that might make an alarm go off, but none did; she exited in silence, emerging at the back of the building, an abandoned block of flats. Everything outside seemed bright and strange, like when she came out of the cinema in the middle of the afternoon.

She had half-expected that when she looked again, Sylvia's body would be gone, like in a film where people who you thought were dead have somehow escaped. She was not in a film though: the body was still there, on the slabs, in its blue suit. Bonnie tried not to look at Sylvia's leg, at the knee that was bent the wrong way.

'Sylvia,' said Bonnie, but she did not really expect a reply.

She looked at the sharp and shiny implement—something surgical-looking, such as a doctor might use—lying near Sylvia's manicured, motionless hand.

Bonnie, crouching, put a hand to Sylvia's throat, and then to her wrist, looking for a pulse. She did not know what to do with the yellow blanket. She wanted to put it like a pillow underneath Sylvia's head, but she felt that she should not move her. She thought that she ought to cover the body, but did not want to put the blanket over Sylvia's face. In the end, Bonnie tucked the blanket around Sylvia's shoulders, leaving the face uncovered, as if Sylvia were only sleeping, with her head on the cold pavement.

Bonnie lit a cigarette, although the shaking of her hands made it difficult, and then she called the emergency services, and they told her to keep the line free in case they needed to call her. She wondered if there would be sirens, or if the ambulance would appear suddenly, quietly.

She found the car and lifted her suitcase into the boot. She was cold in her damp clothes, and had managed to come away without a warm coat, only waterproofs, and they seemed redundant now. She got into the car, sitting at first in the passenger seat, and then shifting across into the driver's seat. She thought of home, of her mother's voice on the phone, and her father's voice in the background; she thought of getting back to work, the amusement arcade and the flashing buttons that said 'GO', 'GO!' An ambulance came around the corner and passed the parked car, and Bonnie saw it slowing down near the block of flats. They would find her.

She checked that she had her cigarettes and her lighter to hand, because she would want them, and then she put the key into the ignition and turned it, waking the engine. She had not driven for years and years, but it was still early, the roads were clear. She held down the clutch with one foot and touched the accelerator with the other and there was a roar. Bonnie released the handbrake and pulled unsteadily away from the kerb, away from the beach, away from the encroaching sea.

Acknowledgements

THANKS TO NICK Royle for prompting me to write the short story 'The Harvestman', a reworking of which became a key part of *Death and the Seaside*, and for the loan of his busker. The UK edition was published by Salt, with thanks to Nick again for his finely honed editing skills, and to Salt's Jen and Chris Hamilton-Emery for their patience and for being, as ever, a real pleasure to work with. Thanks to John Metcalf and Dan Wells for their interest in bringing my work to a North American audience, and to Vanessa Stauffer and everyone at Biblioasis who has worked on this edition of *Death and the Seaside*, including Zoe Norvell for the beautiful new cover. Thanks to Dan for being my other half, for not showing any signs of boredom during the many read-throughs and discussions, for sterling editing and for helping me to find the right ending. Thanks to my son Arthur, for loving stories and for not minding that I sometimes have my head in the clouds. I am also grateful to Andrew Harrison at the University of Nottingham for all his support and encouragement.

I am grateful for the following permissions, and informal blessings, to quote or reprint material:

In chapter 13, the poet heard talking on the radio is Ross Sutherland, www.rosssutherland.co.uk, who was talking on BBC Radio 4's *Short Cuts*.

In chapter 17, I have quoted from *Tricks of the Mind* by Derren Brown. Published by Transworld. Reprinted by permission of The Random House Group Limited.

The Alan Sillitoe story mentioned in chapter 18 is 'A Time to Keep', and the extract is reproduced with the permission of Ruth Fainlight.

The epigraph preceding chapter 21 is from *The Hotel New Hampshire* © 1981 Garp Enterprises, Ltd, by permission of the author and The Cooke Agency.

I have also quoted from *The Lure of the Sea: The Discovery of the Seaside in the Western World 1750–1840* by Alain Corbin, translated by Jocelyn Phelps, published by Penguin; *The Shadow Over Innsmouth* by H. P. Lovecraft; and *The Interpretation of Dreams* by Sigmund Freud, translated by James Strachey. The line 'I am the master of my fate' is from 'Invictus' by William Ernest Henley. The line 'and underneath is everything we don't know and are afraid of knowing' is from D. H. Lawrence's essay 'New Mexico'. The short film *The Death of Tom* is by the artist Glenn Ligon. The 'old silent film' whose intertitles are quoted is *Dr. Jekyll and Mr. Hyde* (Famous Players-Lasky, 1920). Bonnie's reference to the still life by Cézanne is a combination of D. H. Lawrence's description in 'Introduction to These Paintings', *Late Essays and Articles*: 'Walls twitch and slide, chairs bend or rear up a little, cloths curl like burning paper', and the description in *Janson's History of Art*: 'Cézanne took these liberties with reality'. The reference to 'Stan Laurel, who was always in some kind of trouble, some kind of foolish danger' is a nod to Kurt Vonnegut's observation of the 'terrible tragedy' of Laurel and Hardy, who 'are in terrible danger all the time. They could so easily be killed'. The Rough Guide volume mentioned is *Women Travel*. The parkour expert referred to is Daniel Ilabaca, co-founder of the World Parkour and Freerunning Federation. The lines '*My Bonnie lies over the ocean, my Bonnie lies over the sea*', '*Bring back, bring back, oh bring back my Bonnie to me*' and '*Last night as I lay on my pillow . . . Last night as I lay on my bed . . . Last night as I lay on my pillow . . . I dreamt that my Bonnie was dead*' are from the folk song 'My Bonnie Lies Over the Ocean'.

ALISON MOORE'S FIRST novel, *The Lighthouse*, was short-listed for the Man Booker Prize and the National Book Awards, winning the McKitterick Prize. Both *The Lighthouse* and her second novel, *He Wants*, were *Observer* Books of the Year. Her most recent novel, *Missing*, was published in the UK in 2018. Her short fiction has been included in *Best British Short Stories* and *Best British Horror* anthologies and broadcast on BBC Radio. The title story of her debut collection, *The Pre-War House and Other Stories*, won a novella prize. Her first children's book, *Sunny and the Ghosts*, was published in the UK in 2018 and followed by *Sunny and the Hotel Splendid* in 2019. www.alison-moore.com

TELL THE WORLD
THIS BOOK WAS

Good	Bad	So-so